"This place i̇

Emma didn't spe̟
wake the baby.

"We're glad we could help, and none of us expect anything in return." A full minute passed before Tyler added, "Dolly worries you're spending all your time sewing and taking care of Josie."

"I like doing those things."

"Dolly said you haven't had any friends visit since you moved in."

"I haven't had time to meet many people in town."

"You've lived in Lost River for a year, Emma. How long can you shut yourself off from the world?"

"*Aenti* Pearl liked to keep her home serene. That meant no other *kinder* around."

"So you got used to being on your own?"

"*Ja.*" She stood, then collected the plates and carried them to the kitchen. The movement gave her a chance to calm her heart, which was thudding as if she'd run the length of the valley. Because she was talking about *Aenti* Pearl? Or her worry about Gil and Dolly? It was easier to admit those might be the reasons than to acknowledge how her heart had burst back to life when Tyler had put his hand atop hers...

Jo Ann Brown loves stories with happily-ever-after endings. A former military officer, she is thrilled to write about finding that forever love all over again with her characters. She and her husband (her real hero who knows how to fix computer problems quickly when she's on deadline) divide their time between Western Massachusetts and Amish country in Pennsylvania. She loves hearing from readers, so drop her a note at joannbrownbooks.com.

SAVING HER AMISH BABY

JO ANN BROWN

LOVE INSPIRED
INSPIRATIONAL ROMANCE

LOVE INSPIRED®
INSPIRATIONAL ROMANCE

ISBN-13: 978-1-335-93193-1

Saving Her Amish Baby

Recycling programs for this product may not exist in your area.

Love Inspired
22 Adelaide St. West, 41st Floor
Toronto, Ontario M5H 4E3, Canada
www.LoveInspired.com

Printed in Lithuania

MIX
Paper | Supporting responsible forestry
FSC® C021394

But the stranger that dwelleth with you
shall be unto you
as one born among you,
and thou shalt love him as thyself.
—*Leviticus* 19:34

For the wonderful folks at Lickety Split—
Gail, Gina, Mitch and all the other smiling faces.
Thanks for the great food and the friendship.

Chapter One

◁━━◯━━

What was the world record for most yawns in a row? Emma Weaver figured she had to be close.

Being exhausted early in the day wasn't a *gut* thing, but she wouldn't be able to sleep even if she could convince Josie to take a morning nap. The *boppli* had refused to settle down in her crib for the past two mornings, so her afternoon nap had been the only time Emma had been able to concentrate on work. She had to complete a lot of work this week if the shirts and skirts were to be worn during the events surrounding the first rodeo of the season during the second weekend of May. That was a month away. Having an extra hour this morning would have been a blessing, but it didn't look as if it was going to happen.

She glanced out the window of the cabin. To the west, clouds clung to the lofty San Juan Mountains, and their edges were torn by powerful winds high up, where deep snow blurred the edges of the sharp rocks. In the valley, a steady breeze rocked the trees that served as a wind-break behind the house. Would it snow today? In Indiana, she wouldn't have worried about a blizzard in early April, because they were rare. Spring snowstorms weren't as unusual in the high altitudes of the San Luis Valley. She'd thought winter was over when the sun warmed the land up enough over the past week to make the snow retreat. Yesterday, though, temperatures had fallen like a rock cascading from a mountain peak. Overnight, spring had vanished and winter had returned.

If it continued to snow through April in the small town of Lost River, then the season's first rodeo, for high-school and college students, might have to be canceled. The horses and the riders needed solid footing to perform. Or she'd been told. In spite of her commissions to make rodeo wear, she'd never attended a rodeo. During last year's events, she'd been busy trying to get herself and now eleven-month-old Josie settled in.

The cabin, with its one main room and a loft for her sewing machine, was different from the rambling white farmhouse where she'd grown up in Indiana. *Everything* was different from Indiana. The mountains, the weather, the landscape of the San Luis Valley. Maybe the people weren't different, but she hadn't allowed herself to get to know them. Not plain folks or *Englischers*.

It might have been easier to feel at home in

Lost River if her cousin, Sharon Miller, was still with them. The trip west had been Sharon's idea, but when their bus reached a tiny depot outside of Topeka, Kansas, Sharon had abandoned them, leaving a note in Josie's diaper bag telling Emma she'd meet them in Lost River as soon as she could. No other explanation, and, as of today, ten months later, no sign of Sharon returning.

As she had many times before, Emma asked herself why she'd decided to go west with a cousin whom she'd never met before. She'd seldom seen her *daed*'s family after her parents had died, but the answer was always the same. She hadn't hesitated to take her first excuse to leave the place where she'd never felt at home. From the time Emma had been handed over, an orphan at age seven, to her *mamm*'s brother and sister-in-law, *Aenti* Pearl had found fault with everything Emma said and did, as well as what she hadn't done or said. And when *Aenti* Pearl found fault, she lashed out with words and fists. Sharon's invitation to travel with her had been the opportunity Emma had been waiting for.

Now, Emma had to wonder if she was as stupid and gullible as *Aenti* Pearl had labeled her. She was in faraway Colorado, living in a house Sharon had leased, too ashamed of her mistakes to let anyone get to know her and discover how she'd run away with her cousin.

Thou wilt shew me the path of life: in thy pres-

ence is fulness of joy; at thy right hand there are pleasures for evermore. The verse from the sixteenth Psalm was her go-to when everything seemed overwhelming. She hadn't planned to be a first-time *mamm* alone, but she had to believe God had His reasons for putting her on this path.

Josie sat on a rag rug close to the woodstove, trying to stay awake. She'd been up all night because her gums hurt. Walking over to the little girl, Emma ignored the cautionary squeak from the pine floorboards. She'd become accustomed to the cabin's many sounds since they'd moved in last year.

"Time for nap," she said with a lilt in her voice as she scooped up the *boppli*. She never let the little girl see her uneasy thoughts.

Josie curled against her, loving and trusting. *God, a big* danki *for such a small blessing.* As Emma carried the *boppli* to the crib in the cramped bedroom, she drew in Josie's warm, sweet scent. She couldn't imagine a life without the little girl, with her black corkscrew curls blossoming in every possible direction. Her eyes were more gold than brown, like Emma's, and they often glittered with mischief. She'd begun to crawl and pull herself up on the couch. Soon, Josie would be walking—and then running—around the cabin, making it more difficult to work.

Emma tucked the little girl into her crib with

her favorite stuffed toys—a bedraggled teddy bear and a bright pink frog—and tiptoed to the main room. Holding her breath, she listened for Josie's protest. It didn't come, so she went toward the stairs to the loft. Maybe she could finish the embroidered front of the first shirt.

Her foot was on the bottom riser when she heard a knock on the front door. The sound, which she couldn't recall hearing since her first week in the valley, startled her so much her sneaker slid off the step and onto the floor. Not many people drove along Rimrock Road, which was southwest of Lost River. She'd wondered if that's why her cousin had chosen this tumble-down cabin. Or maybe it had been all Sharon could afford.

When the knock came again—louder this time—she rushed to the door and threw it open before the racket roused Josie. Her glasses bounced on her nose, and she pushed them into place.

Her greeting went unsaid as she stared at the tall man standing on her narrow porch. The sun-bleached hair under his straw hat complemented the tan he'd gained from long hours outdoors.

Tyler Lehman!

After church services, she'd heard his name—often in awed tones—on the lips of the unmarried women. Sometimes also from married women who admired his *gut* looks and laid-back attitude.

He was usually with a group of friends, joking. She'd heard he was hard-working, though more than one person had expressed concern about his workplace. Though nobody had stated a plain man shouldn't work in a sporting-goods store, she'd sensed disapproval. She hadn't stayed to eavesdrop on the negative conversation. She'd faced enough censure from *Aenti* Pearl, and she didn't want more in her life—even when it wasn't aimed at her—and not in Josie's. *Kinder* echoed what their elders said.

When he opened his mouth, she put her finger to her lips. "Josie is sleeping."

"Your *boppli* is a girl, ain't so?"

She was about to add that the name should have made that obvious when she noted the twinkle in his blue eyes. "It's a *gut* thing she's a girl when she has a name like Josie."

He faltered as if he hadn't expected her retort. Why should he when he didn't know her? Chuckling, he said, "*Ja*, a *gut* thing."

She put her finger to her lips again. "You must be quiet."

"Sorry," he said in a near whisper. "I'll be quick and quiet. *Mamm* wanted this delivered to you." He gestured to a box beside him on the dusty porch boards. It was as high as her knees. "My *mamm* is Viola Zehr."

"I know your *mamm*." She frowned at the box. "What is it?"

"I don't know. Didn't she tell you?"

"No."

He glanced at the box, then her. "I don't want to open it out here. If it's filled with a dozen large dogs, as it feels it is, they'll pop out and disappear into Far Reaches Creek."

"Dogs?" she choked out, then realized he'd caught her in his jest this time when his eyes sparkled like Josie's. "Bring it in quietly."

"A mouse would be louder than I'll be." He scooped up the box as if it didn't weigh an ounce and carried it through the door.

Thanking him, she went the few steps into the kitchen to give him room to set down the box. She squatted in front of the cupboards that didn't have any doors. Red gingham hung across the openings. Sticking her head into the cabinet to find the plastic tray where she kept her kitchen tools, she picked up her utility scissors. She kept her sewing shears away from paper, not wanting to dull them. That could damage the fabric and fragile threads she used.

She breathed a sigh of relief when she heard the door close. She didn't like being rude, but keeping far from the other plain folk would be the best thing she could do until Sharon arrived and explained why she'd deserted Emma and Josie in Kansas.

No sound from the tiny bedroom. *Gut!* Emma got up, and her gasp erupted when she saw Tyler by the table. The tiny space felt minuscule with him there. His broad shoulders seemed to eclipse the fireplace that didn't work because of a stuffed chimney.

Holding the scissors close to her black apron, she told herself not to be fanciful. The space was cramped. How they'd manage when Sharon arrived was a puzzle she needed to save until later.

For now…

Tyler gave her a scintillating smile, and she struggled to keep from grinning. There was something infectious about his cheerfulness, but *Aenti* Pearl had drilled into her that Emma would be a *dummkopf* to let herself fall for such tactics. *Aenti* Pearl had been right enough for Emma to wonder if the woman's advice about men was sound.

"Do you want me to open it?" he asked, shrugging off his black coat to reveal a light blue shirt and black suspenders underneath.

"I can do it." Her voice was hardened by her shock that he'd made himself at home.

His gaze went up and down her, and she was about to bristle at his boldness when he did the same with the box. He picked it up, then put it on the floor. "You're not tall. It'll be easier for you to open it down here."

"*Danki*, but it would have been okay. We short people figure out ways to do things ourselves."

"Sorry." He held up his hands in surrender. "I didn't mean to step on your toes."

His words sent a wave of disgust over her. Not because of him, but because of her bad manners. He'd traveled out of his way, because her cabin wasn't on anyone else's usual path. He could have dropped the box on the porch and left. Instead, he'd brought it inside and was offering his assistance while she hadn't offered him anything but bile.

"Danki," she said again, then added, "I appreciate your help." She gave him a tentative smile. He wasn't her *aenti*, ready to jump on any mistake, whether real or imaginary.

"Go ahead," he said with a wave of his hand. "Let's see what's in there."

"It may be a dozen dogs."

"Then you'd better hurry. There aren't any air holes in the box."

When she began to laugh, she clapped her hand over her mouth, not wanting to disturb the *boppli*. She ran the scissors along the seam, cutting through the paper and the tape. After putting the scissors on the table, she bent to open the top and gasped as fabric blossomed out like an inflating bubble. She ran her hand down the inside of the box and discovered more and more material.

"There's so much," she said, amazed.

"If I know my *mamm*, and I do," he said with a wink, "she collected from her friends and convinced my sister, Mollie, to do the same with her quilting circle. I hope you can use it."

The top two or three folded bolts were cotton with no pattern on them, but she could see others under them with small prints. She should be able to use it in future projects. What a generous gift!

When she said as much to Tyler, he grinned. "That's how *Mamm* is. She knows what it's like to be a widow, though we were grown when *Daed* died."

"I'm not a widow," she said, then wished she hadn't when his eyes riveted on her. Feeling heat climb her cheeks, she scolded herself. She'd held the truth close since her arrival in Lost River, and she shouldn't be blabbing.

She steeled herself for his next questions about why she was alone with a *boppli*, but he asked, "Where do you want this box put?"

"It's fine right where it is," she said, managing to choke out her reply as she struggled to recapture her composure. The sooner he left, the less likely it would be she'd say something else stupid. "I can unpack the box and take the fabric upstairs. I don't want to keep you from whatever you've got to do today."

"Nonsense." He picked up the box and walked toward the stairs.

Emma wondered if he'd ever, in his whole life, taken a hint to leave, but trailed after him, glad she didn't have to move the cloth up the stairs in multiple trips. She stepped around him at the top of the stairs, taking care not to hit her head on the low, slanted ceiling.

Tyler couldn't stand straight in the loft as he set the box where she indicated. He remained hunched and looked around the space lit by a skylight.

There wasn't much to see. Her zigzag sewing machine sat on a small table with the car battery that ran it underneath, far enough back so she didn't kick it while she worked. Her sewing chair was from a vintage kitchen set, its metal legs chipped, but the yellow vinyl seat was intact. A propane lamp hung from the ceiling, and projects were scattered across her worktable with another lamp, this one run by another twelve-volt battery next to it. Nearly finished clothing hung on a rack pushed as close as possible to the corner where the roof and the railing at the edge of the loft came together.

He walked over to the rack and paused, appraising the fancy shirts and skirt she was working on. Only part of the embroidery was finished, but the threads, laced with sequins, glistened beneath the skylight.

"This is what you do?" he asked. "You sew fancy clothing?"

"Ja." She wished she hadn't sounded so defensive. "I learned how to do sewing-machine

embroidery when I helped an *Englisch* lady in Indiana update her *mamm*'s wedding dress."

"Is that where you're from? Someone told me you lived with an *aenti* in Ohio."

"No. I've lived with *Aenti* Pearl in Indiana since I was seven years old." Not wanting to explain anything more about her past, she said, "That *Englisch* lady recommended me to other clients. My business grew from there. Now, I'm rebuilding it here. Didn't you see my sign when you came in?"

Emma didn't explain how her *aenti* had pushed her to inflate prices for the intricate and time-consuming work. It'd been the worst argument they'd ever had, because Emma had refused to overcharge her customers. From that point until Sharon arrived with her offer to travel west, Emma's life had been horrific. She'd tried to close her ears to *Aenti* Pearl's comments about how ungrateful Emma was after *Aenti* Pearl and *Onkel* Conrad, who'd died when Emma was twelve, had provided her with everything she needed.

Everything but love and respect.

"Your sign?" Tyler asked. "I didn't notice it."

"It's right by the road. You can see it if you look out the window over the front door."

He went to look. She didn't need to, because she'd painted the sign that said, *Sewing and Embroidery and Tailoring Done. Inquire Inside— Every Day Except Sundays*. The lettering wasn't straight, and there were drips of dark blue paint. She'd been in a hurry to bring work in. Though she'd promised herself she'd replace the sign when she had a chance…that chance hadn't arrived. Not since she'd put up a notice on bulletin boards along Lost River's Main Street and work had poured in.

A cry came from below. Emma whirled toward the stairs when Josie shrieked again. "Excuse me. I need to check on the *boppli. Danki* for bringing the box. Please tell your *mamm* I'll thank her at church." She raced down the stairs.

Hoping Tyler *finally* took the hint and left, she rushed into the bedroom. She stumbled over her feet when she saw Josie sitting in the crib and something moving in front of her. Something mottled and serpentine and shaking its tail.

A snake!

Emma screamed.

Tyler stood in the middle of the living room, pulling on his coat. He'd already spent more time here than he'd intended. He was trying to get his mind around what Emma had said. She wasn't a widow. Did she have a spouse, or was she a single *mamm*? It wasn't, he reminded himself, his mystery to solve. He needed to get to work so Monday and Tuesday he could have time off to ski. Reaching for the doorknob, he heard a shriek.

Emma!

Three long strides took him to the bedroom
in a lean-to at the back. It was as cramped as the
loft, but he paid no attention to anything except
the woman who stood at the foot of the bed and
stared in terror at the crib. Inside it was the *kind*
and a snake! It was hissing and puffed up, its head
raised and its eyes focused on the *boppli*.

"Rattlesnake!" Emma cried. "It's going to bite
her!"

He stepped around her and reached into the
crib. Ignoring Emma's warnings, he picked up the
boppli, who regarded him with big, brown eyes
filled with tears. Her finger was in her mouth,
and she was drooling. He handed her to Emma,
then grasped the snake behind its head. He carried it out of the room and to the front door, which
he opened, and then set the snake on the ground.

"Have you lost your mind?" Emma demanded
behind him. "It could have bitten you. Rattle-
snakes are poisonous!"

Facing her, Tyler said, "It's not a rattlesnake.
It's a bull snake."

"Is it poisonous?" Her voice dropped closer to
its normal pitch.

He shook his head. "No. It was—"

"Don't you dare say it was more scared than I
was. That's not possible."

He was amazed when a hint of a smile tilted
her lips. Then he asked himself why he was surprised. Any woman who moved to a different

town in a different state with a *boppli* in tow must possess a large dose of courage.

"Are you okay?" He wasn't sure what else to say.

"I will be." Her eyebrows lowered. "How do you think it got in?"

"They look for a warm place to hibernate. It wouldn't take a big hole for it to crawl through."

"Will it return?" Her eyes widened as she hugged the *boppli* close. "It could be a rattle-snake next time."

"I'll check beneath the house. If there's a hole in the floor, I'll stop it up for you."

"You'd be willing to do that?" Her nose wrinkled. "It's not nice under the house."

"I assumed that. I've lived on a farm my whole life."

The words that once might have seemed comfortable on his lips caused him to flinch. *Ja*, he lived on a farm, but it no longer seemed like home. What a change from last spring when his younger sister and *Mamm* had lived there! *Mamm* had moved in with her new husband a couple of houses along the dusty San Luis Valley road in southern Colorado, while Mollie lived on a ranch about two miles away.

Maybe that was why, every day, he was eager to get to work in the sports-equipment store that was undergoing renovations on Main Street. It was seldom empty and never quiet. Or it could be as simple as working his hours during the end of the week meant he had time off to ski on Monday and Tuesday. He never cared what days he worked during the summer, but once snow began falling in the mountains, he wanted to hit the slopes. Spring was banishing the snow, and this coming week might be his last chance to test his new skis. If he'd been able to take the position on the ski patrol when it'd been offered a couple of years ago… That had been impossible when he needed to remain in the valley to help his family. But with *Mamm* and Mollie now moving on with their lives, it was time for him to do the same.

This wasn't how he'd planned for his day to go. When his younger brother, Kolton, had told him *Mamm* had asked for Tyler to deliver the box to Emma, there could have been only one explanation. *Mamm* was matchmaking again.

She was doomed to failure.

Tyler had no interest in a relationship. He had to know his heart before he could offer it to someone. While he tried to decide if he wanted to remain in the plain community or step over the fence into the *Englisch* world, getting involved with a woman, whether plain or *Englisch*, would be wrong.

If *Mamm* wasn't matchmaking, she could be trying to persuade Emma to become more of a part of the community. With a fabric as bait? If

Emma wanted to become more involved with the *Leit*, she would have.

Emma must be bothered by the speculation about her and her *boppli*. He'd heard a lot after church services. Was Emma a widow? Unmarried? No one had answers, but everybody had an opinion to air.

As they did about him. There had been too many times lately when he'd approached a group deep in conversation to have them grow silent as they turned to regard him with innocuous grins. Why shouldn't a man enjoy a sport along with his *Englisch* friends? A sudden pulse of sympathy for Emma soared through him. He'd learned to ignore the gossip, and she must, too.

Or was she questioning if she should become a full member by being baptized as he was?

Tyler shook that thought from his head.

The *boppli* let out another cry. Had the snake struck her? Even a nonpoisonous snake could bite. He hooked a finger around the little one's hand and drew her finger out of her mouth. A small pinpoint of blood was along one side.

Emma cried out in horror. "It bit her!"

"Looks more like its fang scraped her finger. Bull snakes have pretty small teeth, so they can't bite deeply."

His words failed to calm her this time. She held the *boppli* close and gasped, "What am I going to tell her *mamm*? She trusted me to watch out for her."

"Her *mamm*?" he repeated in disbelief. "Aren't you her *mamm*?"

She stared at him with as much horror as she had the snake. Her answer was soft. "No. The *boppli* isn't mine."

Chapter Two

Emma berated herself, her finger trembling as she pushed her glasses up her nose again. The motion let her hide her face as she tried to regain control of herself.

How could she have been careless? Because the snake had scared her half out of her wits shouldn't have loosened her tongue. Sharon hadn't asked her to hide the truth, but Emma had, unsure why her cousin had left her adorable *boppli* with Emma before she vanished. The only explanation Emma had been able to devise was that Sharon had believed Josie wouldn't be safe with her any longer.

Why?

Was Josie in danger now?

Because she couldn't answer those questions and many more, Emma had been looking over her shoulder, keeping herself apart since she'd reached Lost River, the place her cousin had set as their destination. Worshipping on a church Sunday, dealing with customers, shopping in

town—everything was done with as little interaction as possible.

She stood in the cramped cabin Sharon had
leased for them, Josie in her arms, with Tyler
Lehman staring as if she'd turned as ginger as
her hair. He'd opened his mouth twice to reply,
then seemed to think better of it.

Knowing she owed him an answer and understanding he had more questions, she said, "I
need to take care of Josie's hand. I don't want it
to get infected."

"*Gut* idea." The words came out as if some-
body had their hands tight around his throat.
Something else she could empathize with, because she hadn't taken a deep breath since Sharon had disappeared.

Emma sat the *boppli* on the kitchen counter. First, she washed the *kind*'s hands. After
cutting a small piece of a thick leaf from her
aloe vera plant, she ran a knife down its length
and squeezed. She placed the goo that emerged
against Josie's finger. When the *boppli* started to
put it in her mouth, Emma drew her arm down.

"It's going to taste bad. Yucky." When the little
girl pouted at being thwarted, she added, "Trust
me on this." Making faces at Josie, she distracted
the *boppli* long enough for the gel to harden, protecting the shallow wound.

Tyler handed her a small latex bandage adorned

with rainbows and kittens. "This might convince her to keep her finger out of her mouth."

"Why do you have a bandage like that?"

"I keep them in my pocket for my niece and nephew." He offered her a smile.

Taking the thin piece of plastic, Emma didn't return his smile as she wrapped it around Josie's finger. The *boppli* chortled with delight.

"Danki," Emma said, realizing how many times she'd said that since Tyler had knocked on her door. She hadn't imagined a man who caught the eye of every woman and the ear of every man would be down-to-earth. Was he really, as she'd heard people say, leaving to join the *Englischers*?

"Why do you have a *kind* who's not yours?" he asked.

Emma appreciated the straightforward question, so she gave him a straightforward answer. "My cousin, Sharon, left her daughter with me while we were traveling from Indiana."

"While?"

"Ja." She explained what had happened in Kansas.

"You agreed to her plan?"

"I didn't know her plan." She gave a terse laugh as she lifted the *boppli* off the counter, set her on the rug and pulled the small box of toys closer. Looking at Tyler, she added, "Sharon was scared. I realized that later. She hid her face when people walked past us." She reached out toward him, but splayed her fingers on the dining-room table to keep from touching him as she pleaded, "Tyler, you can't tell anybody what I've told you."

"The bishop—"

"May insist the police be brought in. That could be disastrous."

"Don't you want to know what's happening with your cousin?"

"Of course, I do, but the police could alert the person Sharon's scared of, letting he or she learn Josie is here. I can't risk that." She stroked the little girl's hair. "Sharon left Josie with me, and I must keep her safe."

"Why didn't you turn around and go home?"

Emma fought to keep her face from revealing how much she dreaded that question. Avoiding it had been a primary reason she put a quick end to any conversation. She'd hoped, when she left home with Sharon, that they'd find friends in Lost River. That *she'd* find the friends she'd longed to have, friends like the ones *Aenti* Pearl had forced out of her life until Emma had been as isolated in their small community near Richmond, Indiana, as she was in Colorado.

She'd never endure such abuse again. Sharon had assured her nobody should. Emma had believed her cousin, but lately, she'd begun to wonder if anything Sharon had said to her was honest, or if her cousin saw her as a way to escape her own problems.

When Josie began to whimper again, Emma took that as an excuse not to answer Tyler's question. "It sounds as if someone is ready for a bottle."

Emma returned to the kitchen and opened the small fridge, pulling out one she had made earlier. She reached for a pot to fill with water. She watched the tap as she twisted the knob. The flow was weaker than yesterday.

As if she'd said that aloud, Tyler asked, "Does the water always come out slowly?"

"It's been like this for a while."

He squared those broad shoulders. "Let me check under the house. I can try to see where the snake got in, too."

"Now?" she gasped. "I need to heat Josie's bottle."

"Go ahead."

"Don't you want us to leave the house?"

He gave her a cheeky grin that threatened the stability of her knees. "The weight of one slight woman and a little *boppli* won't make a difference. If it did, the creaks would have already turned into cracks." He started for the door, then paused. "If you could fill a pail with water and put it on the porch, I'll get cleaned up before I let you know what I discovered."

"I will." She was going to urge him to be cautious, but he was out the door before she could say another word. Probably a *gut* thing because she was curious as to why he was being helpful.

Had her fear made her like Sharon? Or was she being paranoid, looking for trouble where there wasn't any? If so, and she was focused on that, she might miss real danger to Josie.

Wiggling from beneath the cabin, Tyler grimaced. Sand, dirt and mud clung to him. His trousers stank, and he wondered if they'd ever come clean. Liquid had pooled everywhere. A stench that made him gag warned him away from dark puddles below the kitchen. The house was set on cement blocks, raising it two feet off the ground. He'd had room to move around, but he'd belly-crawled only one body length under it before backing out.

Emma's worries were justified. Several joists were sagging to the point of collapsing. He wasn't sure who owned the battered cabin, but it was clear no maintenance had been done in a long time. San Luis Valley summers and winters weren't kind to buildings.

If he'd had any idea how complicated things would become this morning, he wouldn't have delivered the box on his way to work in Lost River. He'd been certain Emma wasn't going to ask him to stick around and chat. Before this morning, he'd never said more than a greeting to the red-haired woman who wore gold wire-rimmed glasses. After church services, Emma quickly left.

He shook his head in disgust. As he did, he caught another odor.

Gas!

He leaped to his feet and raced to the front porch. He threw the door open. Seeing astonishment in Emma's brown eyes as she was lifting the bottle out of the pot on the stove, he shouted, "Let's go!"

"Go? Where?"

"Out of the house!" He picked up the *boppli*, not pausing when Josie let out a cry of surprise. Tucking her under one arm, he motioned with the other to Emma. "Now!"

"What…?"

"Outside. We'll talk outside."

When she followed him, he wasn't sure if it was because his anxiety had reached her or because he had the *boppli. The boppli*, not *her boppli.* What a shock! He hadn't imagined he'd learn such a truth. Or was it the truth? He didn't know Emma Weaver, so he couldn't be certain if she'd been honest or was trying to pull the wool over his eyes. If she'd wanted to spin him a tale, she could have devised something more believable than a cousin who'd left Emma with a *boppli* far from home. She could have said it was an orphaned *kind* she was caring for.

When she caught up to where he stood by his

wagon, Tyler's first question was where the gas shutoff was. She took a single step toward the cabin, but he seized her arm.

"Stay away," he ordered. "It's dangerous."

"It's dangerous for you, too."

"I don't have a *boppli* dependent on me."

She lowered her eyes, and he sent up a quick prayer of gratitude that God had sent him the right words to convince her to listen. When he told her to wait by the wagon, she nodded and pointed out where the propane tanks were. He trotted to the left side of the cottage. The shut-off was right where she'd said. He turned off the gas and released the breath he'd been holding since he'd caught the first whiff under the cabin. The breeze flowing from the San Juan Mountains would soon dissipate the dangerous fumes.

"Can we go back inside?" Emma asked as soon as he returned to the wagon. "It's chilly."

Tyler nodded, not saying it'd be cold in the house soon without heat. He opened the door and held it as she hurried inside, then shut it after himself, not wanting to let any warmth out.

"I didn't have time to fill the pail, so feel free to clean up in the kitchen." She sat on the couch. Her motion shifted the cover enough for him to see missing patches of upholstery that revealed batting and chipped wood. It wasn't just the cabin that was falling apart. It was everything.

When Emma offered the warmed bottle to

the *boppli*, Josie put her hands around it as she sucked. The little girl's eyes focused on him. He wanted to give her a big grin or say something to make her offer him a milky smile around the bottle's nipple, but he couldn't. Not when the situation was dire.

He didn't brush the dirt off his clothes. *That* could wait. What he had to say to Emma couldn't. "This house isn't safe for you and Josie." He didn't speak about the trails he'd seen that suggested the bull snake wasn't the only animal taking shelter under the house. Freaking out Emma wasn't his goal. Getting her to listen to *gut* sense was, so he began to list the deficiencies he'd discovered. The broken pipes on the water lines and the line to the septic tank, as well as the slumping floor joists and the reek of propane that had been pervasive. "You won't have heat or light or any way to cook until the line is patched."

"I know." Behind her glasses, her dark eyes couldn't hide her dismay. "I appreciate you checking, Tyler, but the simple truth is that we don't have anywhere else to live. Sharon paid a year's rent in advance. I don't have money for another place."

"You can't stay here."

"Some repairs—"

"It's going to take more than *some* repairs to make this place safe. With the gas off—"

She gasped and jumped to her feet. After shoving the *boppli* into his arms, she rushed past him into the kitchen.

Tyler stared down at the little girl as he held her far enough from his clothing so the crud from under the house didn't get on her. He couldn't remember when he'd last held such a young *kind*. His niece and nephew had been school age when they joined his family after Mollie had married their *daed* last year. Maybe the last time he'd held a *boppli* had been after his sister was born more than two decades ago. He'd been about five, and a *boppli* had seemed huge in his arms. Now, Josie felt small and fragile. How could Emma think she and this little one could continue to live in this house?

The refrigerator door slammed, breaking his fixation on Josie's golden eyes. "What's wrong?" he asked Emma.

"The food in the fridge will be ruined with the propane off." She stared at the door as if she could will the appliance to work without fuel. "I need to have a way to keep *millich* cold for Josie's bottle."

Tyler wasn't surprised Emma's thoughts were focused on the *boppli*. The *kind* was her whole world. He got that. Skiing was his whole world. How many times had he been in the middle of a conversation with someone after church, and his gaze had been caught by the glistening snow in the mountains? His thoughts focused on the hiss of his skis flying through the snow and the powder blowing into his face and the blur of the evergreen trees along the slope. If the job with the ski patrol was offered again, he didn't know if he could turn it down. His younger brother, Kolton, could handle the farm, and his sister and *Mamm* were happy. Nothing but the community was keeping him in the valley. Was joining the ski patrol the life God wanted for him to have? It wouldn't be a plain life, but he could save people.

Tyler had learned not to let others guess the course of his thoughts, because he'd endured enough glowers from people who believed he spent too much time on inappropriate pursuits. *Mamm* had pleaded with him to be baptized and to make a lifelong dedication to being Amish. Tyler had prayed for a way to explain to the whole community that he never felt closer to God than when surrounded by His magnificent unbroken blue sky, ragged peaks and the crystal glow of snow.

It was the same glow he saw in Josie's eyes as she gazed up at him, her tiny fingers clutching her bottle. What hopes, what dreams, did a little *boppli* treasure in her heart?

He didn't see that light in Emma's eyes. They were dull with defeat and despair and fatigue. He wondered when last she'd had the luxury of time for herself. Between her sewing work, the house and the *boppli*, he doubted she found much time for sleeping.

Time… He glanced at the clock on the kitchen wall, though he knew he was super late for work. Then he realized maybe heading into Lost River and talking to his bosses could offer the solution for Emma's problem.

Walking to the counter, he said, "It's cold outside. You can keep food on the porch."

"The wild animals would have a feast." She continued to gaze at the fridge. "I've got to be careful the lid of the trash can is latched on, or they consider it an invitation to dinner."

"Do you have a cooler?"

Her head jerked up, and he saw hope in her eyes. "*Ja*, but it's small."

"Put the most perishable items in it with whatever ice you have. I'll run into town and bring a couple of the large coolers we've got at the store, as well as more ice. That should get you through tonight. After that…" He had ideas, but he wasn't going to make assurances he wasn't sure he could keep.

"*Danki*. Again." The faintest of smiles drifted across her lips.

As he handed her the *boppli*, he wondered how the cabin's temperature could have jumped a half-dozen degrees. The brush of her fingertips against his skin as she gathered Josie close to her pumped up the warmth in him.

She stepped away, her gaze on the *kind*. Had she sensed the same heat when they touched briefly? If so, he saw no sign of it.

When he told her he'd be back as soon as he could with the coolers, she said simply, *"Gut."*

He went to his wagon and got in, turning it toward town. If he had any sense, he'd find someone else to deliver the coolers and wish her well. He didn't have any because his brain was already working on ways to get her a safe and inexpensive place to live. He had no doubt he could find a solution for her problems, but wondered if it'd be as easy to find one for his attraction to a woman who wanted as little as possible to do with him and the rest of the plain community.

Chapter Three

⮑

Emma was unsure why, when Tyler had returned to the cabin last evening with a pair of
ice coolers as big as Josie's crib, she'd agreed
to go into town today. Now, she drew Apricot,
her horse, to a stop in the center of Lost River.
It was a sunny day with barely a breeze, so the
air wasn't chilly. She'd enjoyed the drive from
the cabin, which seemed colder inside than out.
When they'd passed two of the new barn quilts
that had been hung since last year's Fourth of
July, she'd admired them. Josie seemed delighted
by the bright colors surrounding the depiction of
running horses on a barn about a half mile outside of town. Emma preferred the wooden barn
quilt, with its painted columbines, on the town
barn.

She'd had plenty of time to admire the barn
quilts that were part of a valley-wide project. She
couldn't travel quickly in the small wagon she'd
cobbled together from pieces found outside the
cabin. The wagon must have been a pony cart be-

cause it was narrow and not high off the ground. In the bedroom's tiny closet, she'd discovered two benches better suited to a schoolhouse than for use by an adult. After cutting off the legs more than she'd planned because she'd had trouble getting them even, she'd fit them back-to-back in the wagon. That had left enough room at the rear for Josie's stroller. Her best discovery had been a set of four wheels and their connecting axles, which she guessed had once been on a riding lawn mower, though she had no idea why anyone had kept such a machine in a place without grass. She'd affixed them to the wagon after four failed attempts and had purchased a gentle-spirited horse from *Doktor* Lynny Marquez, the local veterinarian. Apricot didn't seem bothered by the oddly sized vehicle. Emma's plan to sew a top had been postponed week after week.

She drew in beside a buggy at the hitching pole on Lost River's Main Street. She shouldn't be in town when she had work to do, but Tyler had been so helpful. She didn't have the heart to tell him she needed to make use of every minute of sunlight. She'd struggled to move the single battery-operated lamp from the loft to the living room downstairs last night after Josie had been tucked in. It was too heavy for her to move back up.

Emma glanced at the clock set in front of the town hall. It was at least eight feet tall and made of cast iron. On top of its pillar, the clock's double faces were more than two feet in diameter. The black numbers and clock hands were topped by "Lost River" in a simple font. It had the appearance of a long-treasured part of the city, but had been put into place last fall in a ceremony to commemorate the town's founding a hundred and fifty years ago.

The clock showed she was a half hour late. She hated being late.

After tying up Apricot, Emma took the stroller out of the wagon and slung her purse strap over her shoulder. It was heavy with bottles and diapers, as well as small toys and a box of teething biscuits.

"We don't pack lightly, ain't so?" she asked the *boppli*, who gave her a ragged grin drenched with drool. Josie's next tooth would be coming any day now.

Emma opened the stroller and put the little girl in it. She looked along the busy street that ran from east to west as if someone had outlined the road with a ruler. The cross streets were perpendicular to Main Street. Only the train tracks cut a slow curve around the town.

Where was Mountain Sports and Adventures? Tyler had assured her she couldn't miss it, but few of the shops and restaurants had signs protruding over the sidewalks. Then she realized why he'd been sure she wouldn't walk past it. *Mountain*

Sports and Adventures was announced in wiggling letters over the door of a building painted an eye-searing purple with turquoise and yellow trim. The front-porch floor had weathered to a dusty gray-brown. Her black sneakers thumped across it as if she was wearing cowboy boots, and the stroller bounced over every uneven board.

Inside, it looked as if a cardboard factory had exploded. Boxes were stacked everywhere, and folded ones were piled on a pallet to her right. Glass display cases had been pushed to the other side, and the ceiling had been torn down, leaving the rafters visible. Unlike the other buildings along the street, the front of this one was a single story. The roofline rose to a second floor at the rear. Spots for skylights had been marked on either side. A *gut* idea, because the interior was dark.

"You'll need this if you're coming in," said a deep voice at her elbow. A hard hat was pressed into her hands. "Don't bump into any boxes. I'm not sure how stable they are."

Looking at a man and a woman, Emma guessed the two *Englischers* were Tyler's bosses, the Yarwoods. The woman was dressed in a flowing, flowery dress that tied at her nape over a long-sleeved orange T-shirt and was draped like a partially inflated balloon. The man, who matched Tyler in height and breadth of shoulders, wore what Emma knew were bicycle shorts—these fluorescent yellow—and a tight shirt of the same color with vivid red slashes across it. Didn't he realize the temperature was still chilly outside? He dangled a bright green helmet in one hand and a metal water bottle in the other.

"You can handle it, Dolly," the balding man said. "I've got to leave now to meet the guys for our ride through the Cochetopa Pass. If I'm late, they'll go without me."

"That's ridiculous, Gil," the dark-haired woman replied and rolled her eyes. "You can't go out with that filthy bottle. Everyone will think we closed the bakery because the health department shut us down."

"Dolly, the bottle isn't dirty. It's the pattern."

Her nose wrinkled. "I don't care. It looks like you dropped it in the mud. If—" She paused and looked past her husband to where Emma stood in the door. "Ignore our bickering. It's our way of discussing new products."

Gil held up the metal bottle that did look as if it'd been splattered with mud. "You're right, Dolly. I don't like this one. Let's look at the others after I get back." Without a pause, he said, "You can call me if you've got any questions."

"If you've got cell coverage…"

He gave her a resounding kiss on the cheek before heading out. She flushed, and Emma looked away. What was her face revealing? How much she'd hoped for a special guy? She'd thought she'd met one in Indiana, but a single meeting with her *aenti* had sent him scurrying away, never to return.

Dolly faced her, wearing a huge grin. "You must be Emma."

"Ja."

She raised her voice. "Hey, Tyler, your friend is here."

Emma kept her smile in place, but it wasn't easy. She barely knew Tyler Lehman. To call him her friend stretched the truth. A pang of yearning swept over her at the thought of having someone she could depend on, as she hadn't been able to rely on her family or Sharon.

Don't be silly, she told herself. She'd trusted in the past, praying each time that this time God had put an ally in her path. She'd been naive, and she'd paid the price each time. She wouldn't do that again. She *couldn't* because she might not be the only one hurt. Josie would, too, and she couldn't let that happen.

When Dolly shouted his name, Tyler stopped counting the boxes from yesterday's delivery. He should have done an inventory then, but he'd gone to Rimrock Road with the ice coolers for Emma. His work today might have gone faster if he could get her out of his head.

She wasn't a widow, and she had a *kind* who wasn't hers. No wonder she kept herself separate from the plain community. He couldn't imagine how those secrets weighed on her slight shoulders. Though he didn't know her, he was certain of one thing. Her inner strength belied her size. Not once, while she'd told him the amazing story of her cousin deserting her and Josie, had she suggested someone should feel sorry for her. Instead, she'd acted as if everybody faced such challenges.

"Coming!" he yelled to his boss.

Had Emma finally arrived? Tucking his turquoise shirt into his trousers, he walked toward the front of the store. He'd begun to wonder if she'd show up today.

He stepped around boxes stacked higher than his head by the interior staircase that led up to the second story. He admired how pretty Emma was, with her ginger hair beneath her white cone-shaped *kapp*. She wore a dark green dress and black apron. Her fragile appearance was an illusion, he reminded himself.

With a nod toward the women, he bent toward a grinning Josie in the stroller. "Hey there, cutie." She wiggled in an invitation for him to pick her up. "No more playing with snakes, I hope."

"No, *danki*, God," Emma breathed with relief. "You scared them away."

"Snakes?" asked Dolly.

"Long story," he replied. "I'll tell you later."

Dolly glanced from him to Emma. "If you need me, I'll be unpacking these ugly water bottles."

"We should send them back and get hard hats for our littlest customers."

With a gasp, Emma asked, "Is it that dangerous?"

He lifted the plastic hat off her head. "This isn't a real hard hat. Just one of Gil's jokes." He tossed it on top of a glass case, then stretched to keep it from sliding onto the floor. "By the end of the week, we'll have these boxes unpacked and displayed."

"Is it sports equipment?"

"Mostly ski and snowboard equipment for next fall." He kept his voice carefully neutral as he asked, "Do you ski?"

"It's not a big sport in Indiana."

He chuckled, delighted she'd given him a light-hearted answer. "You should join me and my friends sometime. We'd be glad to teach you."

"Maybe." Her tone suggested she wanted to turn down his offer, but didn't want to hurt his feelings. "You asked me to *komm* here."

"*Ja*, I did. Follow me." He turned to go through the maze of boxes to the side door, then thought better of it. The stroller might bump into one. "Let's go outside."

"All right." She sounded dubious, and he couldn't blame her. He hadn't explained why he'd asked her to visit the store.

As he reached the front door, he glanced at Dolly, who was smiling at their small procession. She gave him a thumbs-up before continuing to sort the water bottles into two piles she'd earlier described as hideous and not-so-ugly. He guessed most would be returned and new ones ordered. He or Dolly would supervise the order. Gil never paid any attention to colors or style, much to his wife's dismay.

Tyler believed Gil made a mess of everything because he didn't want to be in charge of inventory. Gil preferred to schmooze the customers, leaving details of the business to his wife and more and more to Tyler.

"Wasn't there a bakery in this building before?" asked Emma as she rolled the stroller along the porch and onto the sidewalk.

"*Ja*, the Yarwoods had a bakery for about a year, but they didn't enjoy it, so they decided to change the business into a sport-equipment shop."

"And adventures? What does that mean?"

He smiled, glad she'd asked. "We're going to offer customers the chance to hire a guide for a day or two or three to take them skiing or hunting or sightseeing."

"Who's going to do that?"

"Me, to begin with."

Her eyes widened. "You're a backcountry guide?"

"Why not? Plain folks like camping and hunting as much as *Englischers* do. I won't be leading the bicycling adventures this summer. That'll be Gil." Not wanting to give her a chance to ask another question, he said, "Turn down the alley between this building and the next."

"Where are we going?"

"You'll see."

The space was about five feet wide. Too narrow for most vehicles, but fine for a stroller. Taking a surreptitious look, he was pleased to see her following. He went to a set of stairs that led to the upper floor of the Yarwoods' building. He started up, then waited while she unhooked the *boppli* and balanced her on one hip as she climbed.

He opened the white door at the top. The bare floors inside were covered by a rug that might once have been green or blue, but had faded to gray. The room had windows on both sides as well as two overlooking the street. A sofa and a table with four unmatched chairs were set in the middle. High ceilings were decorated with plaster vines that flowed toward a medallion in the center. The lamp that had once hung there was gone, leaving an empty hole in the middle. However, the paint wasn't chipped, and the window's panes hadn't cracked.

"What's this place?" Emma asked.

"Save your questions 'til the end of the tour." He grinned. "I heard someone say that while walking tourists around Lost River, and I thought it was clever."

She remained somber. "I don't understand why I'm here."

"For now, just look around and keep an open mind." He motioned toward an arch.

On the other side, a kitchen had a sink set into a metal cabinet. A pair of tall cabinets sat on either side of a gas stove. The space where the refrigerator had been was vacant, and what looked like a discarded wood bookcase was set close to a door at the rear.

"It's not fancy," he said.

"I can see that, but why are you showing me this?"

Instead of answering, he led her past a bathroom decorated with light green and black tiles that must be older than his *mamm*'s *grossmammi*. He didn't pause as he opened two doors beyond it. One was a large bedroom. The metal bed frame had been painted white, and the mattress was topped by folded sheets and blankets, with a pair of pillows perched on top like cherries on a sundae.

She peered past him into the other room, which was empty. Sunlight flowed through the window, setting dust motes to dancing in its beam.

"I figured this would be a *gut* place for your sewing machine, Emma."

"My sewing machine?" She stared at him. "Why would I want my sewing machine here? It took me more than a half hour to drive in today, and the weather was nice. Once it begins snowing next winter..."

"I'm not talking about moving just your sewing machine. I'm talking about moving you and Josie."

"Impossible."

He caught her by the shoulders before she could turn away. Holding her so she couldn't evade his intent gaze, he said, "I asked you to keep an open mind."

"There's a difference between an open mind and a mind where common sense falls out."

Instead of answering, he opened a closet door to reveal shelves covered with old shelf paper kept in place with thumbtacks. It was, he knew, as crisp as a potato chip and as easily broken. "This would hold your fabric, Emma. There's room for thread and your other tools. Admit it. This place would be perfect for you and Josie."

He watched her face, seeing emotions fly across it like leaves before a storm wind. She liked the apartment, but was afraid to say so. Why? Because she thought he'd show it to her, knowing she couldn't afford it? His hands closed into fists behind his back. Who had treated her so cruelly she expected everyone to act like that?

"This is huge," she said as she walked into the main room. After opening the door that revealed another door to the interior staircase leading down into the store, she shut it again. She put

Josie on the floor along with a stuffed dog, and the *boppli* giggled, happy to be unconstrained. "It's three times the size of the cabin. There's no way I can afford it."

"Dolly and Gil know that, and they're willing to make it available to you and Josie, anyhow." He smiled and told her the rate the Yarwoods had proposed. "That includes utilities."

"So little?"

"Ja."

She sat on the couch, which gave a warning creak. "Why are they doing this for someone they don't know?"

"They're *gut* people, Emma. They want to help, and you'll be helping them."

"How does accepting their generosity help them?"

"What I'm going to tell you isn't known beyond these walls." He saw her flinch. Did she think he was going to spill a secret he'd pledged to keep? Did she believe that meant he would tell everyone what she'd told him? Taking a deep breath, he quickly added, "Dolly anticipated you'd be loath to accept charity from strangers. She said to tell you that having you here would ease their minds because there have been break-ins along Main Street recently. The equipment downstairs is valuable and easily stolen and resold. Thieves would be less likely to enter the store if they knew someone was in the building."

"Would they be intimidated by a little *boppli* and a woman? Especially a plain woman who wouldn't raise her hand against them?"

"What's important to them is they do their deeds unseen." He pointed to the telephone on the wall next to the kitchen door. "That doesn't work, but they won't know it. Word will get around that you'll alert the police if you hear anything downstairs."

"I might not hear something if I'm sewing."

"Emma, I don't have time for you to give me reason after reason why you shouldn't accept what Gil and Dolly are offering. Neither of them has said anything, but I suspect they're having trouble having *kinder*. When I approached them about you renting this place, they were hesitant until I said you had a *boppli*. Their faces lit with joy, and they urged me to convince you and Josie to move in." He raised his chin, as he'd watched her do. "Don't you want to live where the building isn't going to fall down around you and you have heat and gas to cook, but no slithery visitors?"

She would be a *dummkopf* to turn down such an openhearted offer; yet she hesitated. He waited for her answer, knowing he couldn't make the decision for her.

"Ja," she said in little more than a whisper. "If God has put such kindness for a stranger into

your hearts, then I must not turn down their offer. *Danki*."

He assumed he'd nodded and that he'd said something about arranging to get her furniture and a refrigerator moved in the next day. He must have sounded rational, though his thoughts were revolving around her words about God putting kindness for a stranger into their hearts. He wasn't sure what was in his heart for Emma and the *boppli*, but he suspected it was stronger than kindness.

Was he witless? He needed a way to flush whatever it was out of his heart and hide it away in the same place he kept his uncertainties about committing to a plain life. He liked his life the way it'd been up until a day ago—having fun with his *Englisch* friends and having a job that provided him with everything he needed to escape to the slopes, where the only decision he had to make was which slope to try first.

Chapter Four

Tyler used his hip to push aside the apartment door as he maneuvered his end of a dresser through the entrance at the top of the stairs.

"Slower!" called his younger brother from farther down the steps. "Don't tilt it! The drawers are sliding."

Tyler halted and pressed his arm across the top two drawers while Kolton did the same with the bottom ones. It would have been simpler if they could have carried the chest on its back, but getting it through the door would have been impossible.

He and Kolton were often mistaken for twins because they had the same height, same streaked light brown hair and same square jaw. Their younger sister, Mollie, described them as tall, light and stubborn, and he had to admit she wasn't wrong.

He and his brother might look alike, but they were very different. Kolton was focused on the family's farm while Tyler spent time there only to assuage his guilt at leaving the work to his younger brother. Kolton had taken over the management of the beef cattle and the fields when their *daed* had become ill three years ago, and Tyler was grateful. While most plain men felt they were blessed to spend lives working the land, Tyler had known from the first day he followed *Daed* around that such a life wasn't for him. He liked animals and being outdoors, but not following a team of horses around a field. If he was going to be out in the fresh air, he wanted to be on the side of a mountain with new powder blowing up in his face as he raced down on his skis.

A shorter arm stretched past him, intruding on his thoughts, and Tyler caught the scent of Emma's lilac shampoo. He wanted to drink in that luscious scent, but said, "Step back, Emma. I don't want you getting crushed."

She did. It'd been that way with everything they'd moved. She'd hovered nearby, as anxious about a box of the *boppli*'s toys as about her sewing machine. As she waited without much patience for them to get the dresser inside, he reminded himself—again—to point out she could use one half of the barn beyond the parking area to stable her horse. He'd intended to show her around when they first arrived with her things, but she'd hurried upstairs to get the *boppli* out of the spitting snow. The weather had warmed and dried since then, which he was grateful for.

"Where do you want this?" Tyler asked as he edged the dresser through the door, taking care not to skin his knuckles as they brushed against the molding.

"The sewing room." She backed away from the door and pointed across the cluttered living room. "In there."

He almost told her not to waste her breath because he already knew which room she planned to use for sewing. He'd assumed she'd use the brighter room and bigger room for her bedroom. Instead, she'd had him and Kolton put the pieces of her bed and the *boppli*'s crib in the smallest room. The two pieces of furniture would take up the floor space, so her dresser and the tiny nightstand must go somewhere else.

Once they began to bring in her sewing supplies and equipment, he understood why she'd chosen the larger room for her sewing. He hadn't guessed how many boxes of supplies and tools she had squirreled away in a shed behind the cabin. Now, she could have everything in her workspace and not have to spend time searching for a specific spool of thread or pair of scissors.

Tyler eased the dresser through the interior door, glad it was wider than the one at the top of the steps. Walking slowly so his brother could get his end past the molding, he nodded when Emma told him where she wanted the dresser.

"Whew!" breathed Kolton when they'd set the dresser, drawers intact, next to the window. "Did you pack an elephant or two, Emma?"

"I'm sorry it's heavy." Dismay blossomed in her eyes. "I should have emptied it out and—"

Kolton waved her to silence. "Don't you know that Tyler likes any chance to show off his muscles to a pretty woman?"

Seeing the blush on Emma's cheeks, Tyler wondered if his face was as crimson. He would talk to Kolton later and remind his brother how shy Emma was. Tyler wouldn't say a word about his own reaction. How was he supposed to explain to anyone how he'd learned carefree flirting could lead to heartbreak when his heart wasn't in it one hundred percent and he wasn't willing to take the steps that would allow him to marry?

"How about a break?" Emma asked, again interrupting his thoughts. She set Josie on a blanket on the floor of the main room. "Let's have a cup of *kaffi* and the cake Dolly brought up."

"You don't have to ask twice," he said, and his brother nodded. "Half of the county went into mourning when Dolly closed the bakery."

When Emma disappeared into the tiny kitchen and put water and grounds into the percolator, which had already claimed its spot on a back burner, Tyler dropped to sit on the sofa. The cushions sank down farther than he'd expected, and his knees stuck up so high he could have rested his chin on them.

Kolton sat beside him, stretching his arms along the couch and his legs toward the center of the room. "It's a *gut* thing the move was today," his brother said as he stared up at the cracks criss-crossing the ceiling. "Tomorrow wouldn't have worked."

"Bad weather coming?" Tyler wished he had his brother's ability to gauge the weather. Kolton was more accurate than any newspaper.

"No, the bison are."

Tyler sighed. Telling his brother—again!—he was a *dummkopf* to add a quartet of bison to the farm would be wasting his breath. On this matter, Kolton was adamant. Because Tyler was spending much less time working on the farm, Kolton was turning more fields into pasture. He could have bought more Black Angus cattle for beef. That herd rotated through the pastures near the barns along with the two Holsteins they milked. Bison would have to be kept away from the domesticated cattle. It was going to create more work, and Kolton would expect Tyler's help.

He'd assist his brother, of course, but also was committed to his job with the Yarwoods. Though he wouldn't ever accuse his brother of such sub-terfuge, Tyler had to wonder if buying the bison was Kolton's way of trying to persuade Tyler to return full-time to the farm.

Thinking about that was the last thing he wanted to do. He slid off the sofa and sat on the floor with Josie, who eagerly showed him each toy she was pulling out of a box. He widened his eyes as if he'd never seen anything more amazing than a blue plastic ring until she handed him a red one. While he oohed and aahed over each one, she grinned and giggled.

"Bison, did you say?" Emma came out of the kitchen and stood behind a chair holding two boxes. She glanced at the stove when the distinctive pop of the water against the top of the percolator created a rhythm beneath her words. "I've never heard of anyone raising them. I thought they're wild animals."

Kolton leaned forward, his face alight with excitement. "Ranchers are raising them for meat. It's healthier than domesticated beef, and they're pretty self-reliant when out in pasture. Not many predators would try to take down an animal that size."

"What about a wolf?"

"It's true that wolves are being reintroduced in the state. They've got to eat like every other beast, but I don't want them to eat *my* cattle." He began to talk about the fencing and other measures he'd taken to protect his herd.

When a timer went off in the kitchen, Emma excused herself.

Tyler followed and chuckled when Emma looked up in surprise. "I thought I'd give you a hand," he said. "I've heard enough about fencing and security measures to last me a lifetime."

"He's excited."

"Like Josie with a new toy."

Her smile when he spoke the *boppli*'s name lit the corners of the tiny room. It brightened places in his heart he hadn't known existed, making him feel as if he'd swallowed a twinkling star.

The sensation stayed with him while they enjoyed *kaffi* and some of Dolly's carrot cake. Afterward, he and his brother brought the last few boxes and pieces of furniture upstairs and arranged them as Emma wanted. They put together her bed as well as the crib. Josie had fallen asleep on the floor, and Emma wanted her tucked away before she began unpacking.

Shadows stretched far across the floor by the time they'd emptied the wagon. Days of work were ahead of Emma. Tyler counted more than a dozen boxes in the main room alone. Three times that many were waiting in the sewing room, as well as some in the kitchen and four or five in the bathroom.

"I can get takeout," Tyler offered. "Do you want Chinese or Mexican?"

"You don't have to do that," she replied, and

that bright light within him lost its shine. Her tone suggested she couldn't wait to have them gone.

"I know, but I want to. Would you prefer Chinese or Mexican?"

"Either is fine." Her sigh was so soft, but with fatigue or frustration?

He could have asked himself the same question. He'd enjoyed spending time with her and Josie, but now he wasn't sure what his reaction was to her not-subtle suggestion it was time for him and Kolton to leave. That he didn't have a quick answer added to his annoyance, but he refused to show it as he asked his brother which he'd like.

"Neither for me," Kolton said, heading for the door. "I've got to get home. Chores. Tyler, can you catch a ride home from Gil or Dolly?"

"I'm sure I can. Gil told me they were planning to work late tonight."

"Gut." Kolton nodded to Emma. *"Danki* for the *kaffi* and cake, Emma."

"I'm the one who should be saying *danki* for your help, Kolton." Her smile returned. "I couldn't have made this move without you and Tyler."

"If you need any other help, give a yell." He hooked his thumb over his shoulder. "To Tyler. I'm going to be busy with the bison."

Emma nodded. "I'll be praying everything goes well tomorrow with their arrival."

Tyler wasn't sure who was more surprised when she gave his brother a hug, Emma or Kolton.

Or him.

One thing he knew for certain—he now knew what *he* was feeling.

Envy.

Emma paused the following afternoon and looked around the living room. It was filled with cardboard boxes, but most were now empty. She had the boxes in her sewing room to tackle. She'd deal with them after supper, when Josie had gone down for the night.

Leaning against the wall, Emma rolled her shoulders. She'd taken the shortest of breaks for lunch, and now her muscles were reminding her she wasn't accustomed to reaching into boxes and pulling out items wrapped in newsprint.

How had her life changed so dramatically in such a short time? Two days ago, she'd been living in the cabin in the western part of the valley. Now, she had an apartment in the heart of Lost River. Her head spun when she thought about how swiftly everything had happened.

All because of Tyler Lehman. He'd provided the newsprint and boxes for her move. From reading the company names on the boxes, she knew he must have gotten them from the Yarwoods. That he'd asked on her behalf and they'd agreed were two things she couldn't let herself forget. While she'd gone out of her way to avoid getting involved with people in Lost River, he'd done so much for a stranger.

"What's that verse in Leviticus?" she asked as if Josie could answer her. "The one I used to repeat before bed every night? 'But the stranger that dwelleth with you shall be unto you as one born among you, and thou shalt love him as thyself…'" She'd first heard it in a sermon after her parents' deaths. The words from the nineteenth chapter of Leviticus had stayed with her throughout her childhood, when she'd felt like a stranger in the only home she had.

"Don't be maudlin." Emma had walked away from that life, and letting it follow her across the continent was stupid. Time to get to work.

Before she could move, the phone rang downstairs, the sound crawling up through the floorboards. She frowned when she heard another sound, so soft she might not have noticed it if she hadn't been standing next to the phone on the living-room wall. It echoed the ringing downstairs.

Was the phone connected? Tyler had assured her it wasn't. So why was it making that strange whispering buzz?

When she picked up the receiver and heard Dolly talking, Emma depressed the flap and put the handset in place over the push buttons. It *was* connected, and she'd just eavesdropped on the kind woman who'd given her and Josie a place to live.

Emma faltered. Should she act as if nothing had happened? It wasn't as if she'd heard more than a few words. They hadn't revealed anything about whom Dolly was speaking to or what they were talking about.

No, she couldn't begin her stay in the Yarwoods' apartment by being rude. That could be seen as acting ungrateful. On top of that, she didn't want to embarrass Tyler by failing to admit her mistake. That was no way to repay his kindnesses.

Picking up Josie, who was babbling about the board book she held, Emma made sure the *boppli* and her book were secure before going to a door on the other side of the living room. It opened onto an interior staircase Tyler had told her was fine for her to use if she wanted to speak with the Yarwoods.

A short corridor led to another door. She opened it to discover a narrow landing and the stairs she'd seen from downstairs. Dolly was hanging up the phone at the counter at the rear of the store when Emma rushed down to a medley of creaking steps.

Dolly looked up. Anxiety had dug lines into her forehead. It smoothed with her smile as she waved to Emma.

"How are things upstairs?" asked Dolly. "You

two are as quiet as mice. I don't hear a footstep."
She came around the counter and tapped Josie's
nose. "Hi there, cutie!"

Josie grinned and held out her book.

"Can I look at it?" Dolly took it and began pag-
ing through illustrations as colorful as the bright
red blouse and flowered skirt she wore. "Oh, a
puppy and a pony and a duckie. What a great
book! As cute as you."

Josie took the book and hugged it to her as she
babbled something to Dolly.

"She's got a lot to say, doesn't she?" Dolly
brushed loose strands of hair toward her loose
ponytail. "Such a good baby!"

Emma couldn't be silent any longer. "Dolly, I
need to tell you something."

The shopkeeper's smile vanished. "What's
wrong?" When Emma explained about the phone
and her inadvertent snooping, Dolly grinned.
"Oh, my, Emma! You scared me with your long
face. I thought something was wrong. Like the
ceiling had fallen." She cocked her head and
laughed. "Though I would have heard that, I suspect."

"I didn't mean to eavesdrop."

"Of course, you didn't. You heard something
odd, and you checked it out. I'm glad you did.
One of the reasons we're eager to have someone
upstairs is to keep an eye on the place."

"I heard you talking to—"

"Nobody important. It was a telemarketer making me a once-in-a-lifetime offer that they're sure to call back about at least a dozen times, though I blocked the number." Dolly's voice softened. "You didn't do anything wrong, Emma. Are you okay?"

Emma wanted to assure Dolly she was fine, but she wasn't. *Aenti* Pearl would have been furious. With a shudder she couldn't repress, Emma sat on the bench next to where Dolly had been working. Josie wiggled in her arms, and Emma set her on the floor, watching as the *boppli* crawled along the bench, picked a spot and hauled herself to her feet. Seeing the little girl's triumphant smile, Emma forced her shoulders to relax.

"Emma?" prompted Dolly.

"I'm okay." She managed a tremulous smile. "I may not look it, but I'm going to be fine."

Dolly scooped up a delighted Josie, then sat beside Emma on the bench. "I'm sure you will. Any woman who moved halfway across the country and then lived way out away from everyone with a little baby can handle anything. Don't worry."

"*Danki*—I mean, thanks."

"I've been around Tyler enough to know what *danki* means. Want one?" Dolly pulled a wrapped chocolate-chip cookie out of her skirt pocket.

"You know I can't say no to your delicious treats."

"That was the whole idea."

"Was?"

Dolly's smile wobbled. "When we had the bakery."

Sorrow rushed up through Emma. "You sound sad that the bakery closed."

"It was the right decision for us, but I do miss it." She sighed. "It was a good business for me, but not for Gil. He felt he couldn't contribute anything. He was useless at mixing batters and doughs. I thought he'd enjoy kneading bread. It bored him, and he complained about the stickiness on his fingers."

She took a bite of the soft cookie with the perfect balance of dough and chocolate chips and walnuts. "I thought the reason you closed was…"

"I know what you've heard. That I wasn't a morning person, so running a bakery was a bad match." She sighed. "I don't know where that rumor started or how. Gil and I tried to halt it, but once it gets going, gossip has a life of its own."

"You're working morning and night, so anyone should see the rumor wasn't true."

Dolly wagged a finger. "Don't you know what the gossips will say? That I've changed. They'll never admit they were wrong."

"True."

"It's like that among the Amish, too?"

Emma laughed. "*Ja.* We even have a name for it. The Amish grapevine. It's a *gut* description for how truth can be twisted. Though the

Amish grapevine is also a source of honest news as well."

"That makes it complicated, doesn't it?"

"It does, but it's also a warning that we need to heed whatever we hear with a grain of salt. Otherwise we'll never sort the truth from mixed-up tales."

Crossing one leg over the other, Dolly bounced Josie on her right foot. "Thanks for the excuse to sit for a moment."

Emma saw there were more unopened boxes here than she'd faced upstairs. How much more stock did the Yarwoods need before they could open? The shelves were empty, but bicycling and hiking equipment leaned against the wall. That inventory had to have been a huge investment, and she guessed it needed to be sold quickly, so the Yarwoods could recoup their investment.

"If there's anything I can do to help..." she began.

Dolly asked, startled, "Don't you have enough to do upstairs?"

"I've become an expert at opening boxes. I'd be glad to help you."

"Thanks, but you've got enough on your plate now." She lifted Josie off her foot and handed her to Emma. "We've got Tyler to help most days."

"His brother is getting a big delivery today."

"I heard." Dolly rolled her eyes. "You can be certain Tyler won't spend a minute longer around livestock than necessary. He's not a cowboy by any stretch of the imagination."

"I'm willing to help if you need an extra set of hands. I don't know how to work the cash register—"

Dolly laughed, the sound light, but heavy with fatigue at the same time. "We've never had a cash register. For the bakery, we had just a computer and a box to hold receipts. Nobody uses cash for purchases like sports equipment." She leaned back against the bench. "I shouldn't say nobody. Occasionally we have a cash customer, and I'll hope I keep enough in my purse to cover any change I need to make."

"I've had several tailoring customers ask if they could pay me without cash or a check. I had to tell them I couldn't do that because I didn't have the equipment or know-how."

"It's simple." Dolly rose and motioned for Emma to follow her along the long counter, to where a computer screen was set. "Would you like to learn?"

"If I can help you, *ja*. I doubt I could use it for my business."

"Why not?"

"Isn't it expensive?"

Dolly gave her a wry grin. "One thing you need to know about us, Emma, is that if any aspect of running the business is expensive, you won't see it here. What we sell is expensive. *How* we sell it isn't. Otherwise, we'd be out of business before we start."

When the other woman began to explain how she used the computer to check out customers, Emma listened, fascinated. The system was simple, with every scenario plotted out on the screen. All she had to do was touch the proper box, and the computer did the rest. She was amazed when Dolly explained the low cost of each transaction.

"You have Wi-Fi upstairs if you want to install the equipment." Dolly faltered. "Or are you forbidden from using such technology?"

"I can for business." Emma tapped her chin. "I might need permission from the bishop to have it in my home, however."

"Jerek Stahl is a reasonable man." Her smile became a frown. "Or so I hear. Tyler hasn't said much about your bishop. I get the feeling he likes to keep off his radar since the ski patrol offered him a job. Not Jerek! Tyler!" Her laughter returned.

Emma didn't reply. Was Tyler trying to avoid the bishop? Maybe because of an offer from the ski patrol. Wait a minute! Didn't ski patrols work at resorts in the mountains? Was Tyler planning on leaving Lost River? She wasn't sure how she felt about that, as she wasn't sure how she felt about anything to do with him.

Slapping her hands on the counter, Dolly said,

"Back to work. I'll have Gil disconnect the phone so you don't have the noise."

"Danki." Her smile became more sincere. "You and Gil are so kind to us."

Dolly waved away her words with a hand. "You're doing us a favor by being in the building when we can't. It's making it much easier to sleep."

"Don't you live over the barn out back?"

"No. Our house is a couple of blocks away. Over on Calle Ancha."

"I saw lights upstairs in the barn last night."

"Gil has a workshop for his bicycles up there." Her mouth tightened. "Every night lately he's been getting ready for a long-distance ride."

Emma bit back repeating her offer to help Dolly. Entwining her life more tightly with the Yarwoods, and with the Lehmans, as well, would open her up in ways she couldn't afford. She'd tried to get close to her *aenti* and her *onkel*, and that had been a disaster. She had escaped those circumstances, and she wasn't going to walk into the same. She'd find a different way to repay Tyler and his friends.

Some prices were too high.

Chapter Five

❧

"They're adjusting better than I'd expected." Tyler leaned on the gate in the new fence his brother had installed around the fields where the bison now grazed since their delivery last week. "I still get surprised each time I see them at how big they are."

Kolton nodded. "Big and nowhere near domesticated. That's why I've posted warnings along the fences."

"You don't need a kid deciding to see how the buffalo and antelope play."

His brother didn't smile at Tyler's weak joke. "Technically they aren't buffalo. They're bison."

"I thought the names were interchangeable."

"Lots of people use them that way, but buffalo are from Asia and Africa. Like water buffalo. Bison are native to North America. Bison have those humps and big heads. Buffalo look more like our domesticated cattle."

Tyler arched his eyebrows. "I should have guessed you've learned from those books you've had your nose stuck in. Aren't some of them published by the National Buffalo Association?"

Kolton smiled. "True."

"Will these bison or buffalo or whatever you want to call them require a lot of attention?"

"Not as much as you'd think. I put in stronger, higher fencing to keep them in the pastures. Otherwise, they're independent."

"You'll keep them separate from the beef cattle and the milkers?"

Kolton nodded. "There's plenty of pasture. I'm not a potato man like many around here. Field crops are too vulnerable to the unseasonable storms we get here." He glanced to the east. "The farmers already planting their potatoes are making a mistake. Winter isn't done with us yet."

"Really? If feels like spring."

"Not yet. You'll see."

"So says the guy with his finger on the weather's pulse."

"It's not that difficult if you keep a close eye on the clouds and animals."

"Not difficult for you, you mean."

"Nonsense. You've got a keen sense for knowing when the mountains are getting fresh snow."

"True."

Kolton pushed himself away from the fence. "How much longer will there be spring skiing?"

Tyler faced his brother and decided to be blunt.

"Are you asking when you can count on me to give you a hand?"

"No. I know you don't want to work here. I—" Kolton looked past Tyler toward the road.

Tyler glanced behind him and was surprised to see a horse turning into the drive by the white farmhouse where he'd grown up with his brother and sister.

"Isn't that Emma Weaver?" he asked his brother. "Looks like her weird little wagon. What's she doing here?"

"I don't know."

Tyler loped toward where Emma was getting out of the wagon. Her bright purple dress and black apron fluttered in the afternoon breeze. She held up her hand to shade her eyes from the bright sun as she scanned the barns and fields. He thought of the pictures he'd seen of pioneer women standing straight and peering off into the distance. How easy it would be to imagine her daring to tame this untamed land! Easier because he'd seen the primitive conditions where she'd lived on Rimrock Road, not once complaining about the rough life she lived with her little girl.

Josie! Where was Josie? He'd never seen Emma without her. His pace increased. Then he saw her face was grim with worry, and he was at a run by the time he reached her.

"What's wrong?" he asked in lieu of a greeting.

"Gil has gotten hurt during a bike ride up Slum-something Pass." Her voice shook on each word.

"Slumgullion Pass."

"That's the one."

"How's Gil?"

"I'm not sure. He's at the medical center in Lake City, and it's at least two hours by car." She took a step toward the wagon. "*Komm mol*. We need to get back, so Dolly can go."

"Why hasn't she left already?"

"Because of that big delivery that's coming this afternoon. She wants someone there when it arrives. I told her I could wait for it, but she wants you to sign for it. I didn't ask her what's coming, but you probably know."

"*Ja*. It's the rest of the skis and snowboards and snowshoes she got on a great year-end deal."

"Can you *komm*? Right now?"

Instead of answering her, he yelled to Kolton that he'd return as soon as he could. Emma was in the wagon and holding the reins by the time his brother acknowledged him. Tyler wondered why he was surprised she intended to drive instead of letting him. This was a woman who was used to doing things for herself.

She shared what little she knew about Gil's accident. "His tire caught in a rut or a pothole. He went over the handlebars. Hard. He managed to call for help on his cell phone, but they were taking him for X-rays when they called Dolly."

Tyler bent his head in a prayer for his friend. If Gil had broken something or had internal injuries, the full burden of getting the store open would be Dolly's.

"Amen," murmured Emma beside him.

He raised his head to see tears in her eyes. Not a single one fell. Again, he knew he shouldn't be surprised. Emma Weaver might look as fragile as a wisp of dandelion fluff, but she had hidden depths of steel. No, not hidden. His first impressions had steered him wrong. He'd thought she was standoffish, but she was, instead, shy and dedicated to providing a life for the *kind*.

"Where's Josie?" he asked at the thought of the *boppli*.

"I left her with Dolly."

"I didn't think you'd ever let her out of your sight." He wanted to pull back the words as soon as they burst past his lips.

"It's an emergency, Tyler."

Was everything he said today doomed to be the wrong thing? He couldn't let his annoyance with his inability to decide on the life he wanted make him say one foolish thing after another. For now, he needed to focus on his friends and pray that Gil's injuries were slight. He couldn't be distracted by other things, most especially not by the kindhearted woman sitting beside him.

* * *

Emma had her ears cocked toward the phone on the counter and was keeping a close eye on Josie, who was asleep on a quilt on the floor, surrounded by her toys. At the same time, Emma held a list and checked off the boxes in the tall stacks on the pallets that had been delivered as Tyler read the number on each one. He then pulled out the contents of each one and counted it. Paying attention to the number of red snowboards or the quantity of skis of a certain length wasn't easy. Dolly had left almost four hours ago, promising to call them as soon as she had an update on Gil. How much longer could it take?

She hadn't realized she'd said the last aloud until Tyler answered, "A half hour. No more."

"How can you be sure?"

He pointed to the three stacks. "That's all we've got left to count."

"I wasn't talking about the inventory. I'm wondering how long it'll take before we hear from Dolly."

He glanced at the clock on the wall. The storage space was half the size of the display area of the shop, but none of the enticing decor out front had been wasted there. Raw boards were stained from dampness and age. Metal shelving would hold the overflow stock.

"It should be anytime now," he replied.

As if on cue, the phone rang. Emma turned

to run out to get it, then edged to the side to let Tyler past her. The Yarwoods were his friends, and he should hear the news first.

She listened as he said, "Dolly! *Gut* to hear your voice. How is Gil?"

Every inch of her yearned to stay and listen, but she scooped up Josie and the blanket. A ball fell out of one end, bouncing across the floor. When she went into the front, Tyler was leaning on the counter, taking notes as he kept saying *"ja"* and "okay" to whatever Dolly was saying. He didn't notice her as she slipped up the stairs and into her apartment.

After tucking Josie into her crib, Emma went into the kitchen and put on the kettle. She opened the cupboard and got out the apple pie Dolly had brought up yesterday. She cut two pieces, then set them on plates. Once the kettle was boiling, she set tea to steeping in two cups. She carried them to the dining-room table. By the time she'd retrieved plates and a pair of forks, there was a quiet knock at the door.

"*Komm* in," she said after she'd opened it. "How is he?"

"He's alive, but badly banged-up."

"How badly?"

"A broken right arm, three cracked ribs on that side and a broken left leg." He didn't wait for an invitation, but walked to the table and picked up one of the cups. "Tea?"

"*Ja*. It's bracing and calming at the same time."

He nodded and sat after she did. Setting the cup on the table, he asked, "Do you have any spare *millich*?"

"Always." She got up and went to the refrigerator. She brought the carton to the table, then set it and a spoon next to his cup. "With a *boppli* in the house, *millich* is vital." Folding her arms on the table, she asked, "How's Dolly doing?"

"She's vacillating between being grateful he wasn't hurt worse and wanting to slap him up aside the head for taking such risks." He sighed as the steam from his cup washed up over her face. "She did say that she was staying in Lake City until at least tomorrow because Gil is being kept in the hospital for observation. They want to make sure he didn't do any other damage to himself."

"It's *gut* they're being cautious. What does she want us to do?"

His head snapped up. "Us?"

"You need my help, ain't so?"

With a sigh, he nodded. "Forgive me, Emma. I'm on edge. Dolly has been worried about Gil taking unnecessary chances on his bike, but I'd convinced myself he knew what he was doing. She was right, and I was wrong."

"Nobody was right or wrong. It was an accident." She put her hand over his on the table.

"Nothing either you or Dolly thought had any impact on it. God's will doesn't work that way."

"You sound sure."

"The only thing I'm sure of is how glad I am he wasn't hurt worse."

"On that, we agree." He put his hand over hers.

Her breath caught as the heat from his skin surged along her fingers. Trying to act as if nothing out of the ordinary was happening, she withdrew her hand from under his and reached for her fork as she said, "I hope you like apple pie."

"One of my favorites. Did you bake it?"

She laughed, struggling to make her equilibrium return. "Dolly did, so you know it's going to be delicious."

While they ate, conversation faded. She was grateful because she needed to submerge those unexpected sensations that had swept over her at the brush of Tyler's fingers on her hand. It had meant nothing more than he needed to reassure himself when his friend had been injured. She tried to convince herself of that, suspecting she'd overreacted, but she kept thinking of how warm his touch had been and how simple it would have been to fall into his gaze. It had shown care and concern and eagerness for a solace that she'd longed to offer.

Don't be a dummkopf, she warned herself. He'd been upset, and she'd been nearby. A handsome, charismatic man like Tyler Lehman could have his choice of any woman who caught his fancy. He wouldn't select someone like her. Someone whose life was an utter mess, far from family and friends in Indiana with a *boppli* who might be snatched away at any second.

Stop it, commanded her stronger self. *You take care of yourself and Josie, and you've faced every challenge with God's help. There's no reason to believe that will change, whether or not Sharon returns.*

Tyler's voice intruded on her thoughts. "Speaking of Dolly…"

Had they been talking about Dolly? Emma replayed their conversation before she'd become mired in her thoughts. Oh, they'd been discussing Dolly's pie.

"Dolly was wondering if you'd be interested in working for her," he continued.

"Of course. I told her I'd be glad to help whenever she needs me."

"This is different. She'd like you to sew for her."

Her eyebrows rose. "If Dolly wants me to sew for her, why doesn't she ask me herself?"

"She doesn't want you to feel you've got to agree because you feel beholden to her." He set his fork on his empty plate.

"I am beholden to her. To her and to Gil and to you. This place is safer for the *boppli*." She didn't speak Josie's name, not wanting to waken her.

"We're glad we could help, and none of us expect anything in return." He seemed about to add more, but halted himself. A full minute passed before he added, "Dolly worries you're spending all your time sewing and taking care of Josie."

"I like doing those things."

"She said, and I quote, 'Emma shouldn't be working twenty-four-seven.' Dolly said you haven't had any friends visit since you moved in."

"I didn't realize she was keeping such a close eye on me."

"How can she not? Your outside stairs go right past the store's side window. She sees everyone who goes up and down."

"I haven't had time to meet many people in town."

"You've lived in Lost River for almost a year, Emma. How long can you shut yourself off from the world?"

She looked at her lap. Tyler had an uncanny knack for putting his finger on the truth. If she told him about how her *aenti*'s endless scolds had continued to ring in her ears at full volume for months after she left Indiana, would he think she was exaggerating? Old habits were harder to leave behind than her *aenti*, and she'd forgotten how to make and keep friends.

Deciding a first step might be honesty, she said, "*Aenti* Pearl liked to keep her home serene. That meant no other *kinder* around."

"So you got used to being on your own?"

"Ja." She stood, then collected the plates and carried them to the kitchen. The movement gave her a chance to calm her heart, which was thudding as if she'd run the length of the valley. Because she was talking about *Aenti* Pearl? Or her worry about Gil and Dolly? It was easier to admit those might be the reasons than to acknowledge how her heart had burst back to life when Tyler had put his hand atop hers.

When she returned to the table, he was draining his cup. She had to say something, but not about her past. "Were those your brother's bison you were looking at out in the field?"

"Ja, they were delivered last week, and they're getting used to us while we try to get used to them." He stood, picked up his cup and hers and carried them out to the kitchen. "Four head for now, but Kolton already is imagining a great herd grazing there."

"Your brother's got big dreams."

"More big dreams than one man can fulfill in a lifetime."

"That's *gut,* ain't so? Think how sad it would be if our dreams ran out."

His eyes widened. "That doesn't sound like the ever-practical Emma Weaver I know."

"Then I guess you don't know me that well."

She meant her words to be teasing, but they dropped into an abrupt well of silence. When

Josie let out a cry from her crib, Emma was glad for the excuse to rush out of the room.

What was it about Tyler that made her feel as if she'd known him for years? She didn't know him any better than he knew her, and if she had an ounce of sense, she'd keep her past to herself. No, she'd keep it buried as she had for the past year. The thought of her *aenti* filled her with trepidation, anger and other emotions she shouldn't be feeling.

Like how much she wanted to spend more time alone with Tyler.

Chapter Six

It amazed Tyler how easily he and Emma fell into an unvarying daily pattern over the following week. He came every morning, except Sunday, to work at the store, but he found the door locked because neither Dolly nor Gil was there. Gil's injuries were complex and his leg required surgery, so he'd been kept in the hospital for five days. When he got home, he wouldn't be allowed to leave the house. Even his physical therapist would come to see him. Dolly was staying with him while Emma did what she could to take her place at the store.

They'd worked together in the mornings before Emma went upstairs for Josie's nap and several hours of sewing. She'd returned downstairs with a snack for the three of them later. While they'd enjoyed the break, they'd played with Josie, who had taken an instant delight at how Tyler played peek-a-boo. A couple of more hours of work followed by a quick meal, reheated from something one of their neighbors had delivered, and more sorting and shelving after Josie was put to bed. The doors at the top of the interior stairs were left open so they'd be able to hear the *boppli*.

The pace was exhausting, but Tyler believed the store might still open as the Yarwoods hoped, shortly after the rodeo next month. More than once, he'd fallen asleep on the way home and was grateful his horse knew the way. Most nights he woke up when they reached the farm, but last night he'd slept in the buggy until a biting cold wind had roused him at dawn.

"You don't have to look so chipper," he grumbled to Emma, who was humming a light melody as she folded garish bicycle shorts and put them on a table in the middle of the shop.

"You don't have to sound so grumpy." Her smile eased the sting of her words. "Did you get up on the wrong side of the bed this morning?"

"No, the wrong side of the buggy."

"What?"

He explained as he continued to sort hiking boots by size, and her smile fell into a frown.

"You have to get more rest," she said as if he was no older than Josie, who was chewing on the head of a rag doll. She then tossed it into the air and chortled as it hit the blanket where she sat.

"And you don't?" He tried to keep the irritation out of his voice. Not at Emma, but at Gil, who'd dumped several cases of trail boots into one big box, mixing up sizes and styles.

"I don't have an hour commute to and from work each day. If you need to get here later or leave earlier, I can pick up the slack."

He shook his head. "You've already got enough on your plate with taking care of Josie—"

"Which you do, too."

"I *play* with her. You take care of her, and then you make us meals and do your sewing." He frowned. "You never said what you're sewing for Dolly."

"Square-dance costumes for her and Gil."

"Square dancing?" He gave a terse laugh. "Gil won't be doing that for several months."

"True, but she wants him to attend events with her. She doesn't want him housebound." Emma's eyebrows rose above her glasses. "Dolly likes to manage people's lives, ain't so?"

"You've just noticed that?" His chuckle was more genuine as he matched up the last of the boots in the box and set them on the lowest shelves. "Her heart is in the right place, but she believes she knows what is best, and she doesn't hesitate to tell us."

"Like when she said you were foolish not to take a job with the ski patrol?"

He halted as he was about to reach for another large box of boots to start the match-up process over again. "How do you know about the ski-patrol job?"

"Dolly told me about it last week. It'd be the

perfect job for you because helping people makes you happy." She looked up at him, then away, as if she didn't want him to see the gratitude that rang through her voice. "As I know well."

"Helping others is what we're supposed to do, ain't so?" Could he change the subject?

His pause while he thought went too long because Emma asked, "Do you know Dolly's worried you might accept the job if it's offered again?"

"The ski patrol?" He shrugged.

She must have believed the action displayed indifference because she turned away to offer Josie a teething biscuit and tie a bib under her chin.

Tyler looked into the box in front of him. Nobody knew how much he'd wanted to accept the offer from Nick Bakke, the head of the ski patrol at Bison Springs. The resort west of the valley in the San Juan Mountains was Tyler's favorite place to ski. He and his friends enjoyed backcountry skiing among the sharp peaks, staying alert for avalanche dangers. He never felt more alive than while speeding down a mountain, flanked by tall pines below the tree line. When Nick had approached him after *Daed*'s diagnosis and had asked if he'd be interested in a job the following winter, Tyler had been thrilled to have his dream put right into his hands.

He shook his head as he bent to pick up more boots. The job had been right, but the timing wrong. No, it'd been more than that. His family had been smothered in grief in the wake of discovering his *daed*'s illness, chemotherapy and radiation and his death two years ago. Tyler couldn't have announced then that he was leaving and taking an *Englischer*'s job.

That had been over three years ago. Nick had hinted several times since then that if Tyler was interested in a job, all he had to do was let Nick know. Then what? If the offer was made again, Tyler wasn't sure what he'd do.

Everyone Tyler had attended school with had taken baptism classes, stood in front of the *Leit* and made a covenant with God and the community. Not just the two boys who'd finished school the same year he had, but every student who'd been in the building that year, from the first-graders through the eighth-graders. Kolton had been baptized before *Daed* died, and Tyler had known *Daed* and *Mamm* had prayed he'd take the same step.

"It's okay to wonder what you'll do if there's another ski-patrol opening," Emma said from where she was kneeling by Josie.

He flinched. "Were my thoughts that obvious?"

"*Ja*, because I know it's what I'd be thinking about if I had the opportunity to have the perfect job. I'd be wondering what I'd do if it were offered again."

Tyler walkied to where she and the *boppli* were on the blanket, then sat and faced Emma. "I shouldn't wonder. I should know."

"What makes you think that?"

"Shouldn't a man know what he wants to do with his life by the time he's my age?" He shook his head when Josie held out the soaked teething biscuit to see if he wanted a bite. She stuck it in her mouth and grinned.

"You can't be more than a couple of years older than I am," Emma said, drawing his attention to her. The compassion in her brown eyes threatened the barriers he'd built to keep his heart untouched until he made the decisions he had put off so long.

"I'm twenty-five."

"I'm twenty-two, and I don't know what I want to do with my life other than be the best possible parent I can be for Josie." She gave a tight laugh. "A year ago, I couldn't have imagined that would be my perfect job. Josie hadn't been born, and I hadn't met my cousin. Things change. We've got to change with them, ain't so?"

"Some things change. That's true, but other things don't."

"Life is about change and challenges and how we deal with them."

He grimaced. "That's a pretty pessimistic point of view."

"I see it as optimistic. Change met and challenges overcome. Isn't that a positive way of looking at things?"

"If you can't be sure you can meet every challenge."

"I can at least try."

"True." He leaned toward her, holding her gaze. "Emma, you've worked to learn how to sew well since you were a kid. *Gut* for you, because sewing is a proper job for a proper plain woman."

"You've got two jobs. Helping on the farm and working here at the store. Isn't that what a proper plain man does? Help his family and friends?"

"Maybe, but a proper plain man wouldn't be questioning at my age if he should be baptized."

She folded her arms in front of her and raised her chin, looking as determined as Josie when she had her heart set on a specific toy. "Who says?"

"What?"

"Who says?" she repeated. "Who made such a rule? God? The *Leit*? Or you?"

Taken aback by her questions, he stared at her. He'd seen her in such a pose only a few times. Each time it'd been aimed at protecting Josie, but the *boppli* was happy gnawing on her teething biscuit. Now, she was glaring at *him* like a little dog confronting a big one.

Not that he felt like a big dog. When doubts overwhelmed him, he would have described himself as a rabbit. Scurrying in every direction in a frenzied panic whenever any other creature came near.

"Are you baptized?"

"*Ja.* When I was sixteen."

"That's early."

"*Aenti* Pearl didn't believe I should join a *rumspringa* youth group, that it was better for me to stay home." She made the statement with dull acceptance, and he thought of the other times she'd referred to the woman who'd raised her. On each occasion, her voice had lost emotion. Because she didn't want to show how much she missed her *aenti* or how much she didn't?

Tyler realized with a shock that he had no idea how her parents died or if her *aenti* was alive. Was Pearl married or a spinster? Emma hadn't spoken of an *onkel* or anyone but her *aenti*. When Emma had moved from the cabin to Lost River, her sole concern had been her cousin not being able to find her. She hadn't mentioned a single word about her erstwhile guardian.

"Is the ski patrol the reason you're hesitating to be baptized?" she asked when he didn't answer.

"Not the only reason." His reply surprised him, then he realized nobody had asked him the question directly before. His family had nudged him toward baptism by reminding him he must be baptized before marrying and that he was old enough to want to have a say in the unwritten rules in their *Ordnung.* His *mamm* had pointed out how happy his sister was with her new husband. Nobody had bothered to ask him what was keeping him from making the decision that seemed simple for others. "I want to choose. I know I need to."

"You don't want to make the wrong choice." Her voice was filled with kindness and sincerity.

"*Ja*. If I don't get baptized, I'll always be an outsider. If I do get baptized, I can't change my mind without being put under the *bann*. Then I lose my family."

"That's not true, Tyler. You can see your family."

"But not eat at the same table with them. I couldn't accept anything from their hands, not even a plate of food. That would break my *mamm*'s heart." He paused to take a deep breath. "I know it would have broken my *daed*'s as well."

"Have you asked yourself if you're more comfortable among the *Englisch* or among plain folk?"

"I've asked myself that and a thousand other questions. Each time I do, the answer's the same. I don't know."

"It seems as if you're doing the right thing now by not committing to a decision, one way or the other." She put her fingers on his forearm. "I'll pray for God to guide you."

Or that's what he assumed she'd said because, to his ears, her voice broke up like bad reception on the radio he and Kolton had hidden in the barn when they were teens. The gentle pressure of her fingertips on his sleeve sent reverberations of sensation through him, each tremor heading to his brain, knocking it off-kilter.

Her warm, brown eyes offered him a haven. Not an easy haven, he knew, because she could be as fiery as her hair when she believed Josie needed protection. How had she doused those powerful passions while living with her overbearing *aenti*?

An image burst into his mind of Emma letting her real self free. Her snapping eyes and expressive mouth were close to him. Deliciously close…

No, he couldn't think of such things. He couldn't allow himself to imagine bending his head to capture her lips. Not while he questioned his whole future.

Emma had put down Josie for her afternoon nap the following day when a knock on the door echoed through the apartment. Leaving the bedroom door ajar, she considered slipping into her sewing room and pretending she wasn't there. She needed to put Josie's nap time to the best possible use to finish the rodeo clothes and get a *gut* start on the square-dancing outfits for Dolly. She'd promised Dolly to have the clothing finished within a month, and she intended to meet her deadline.

The idea of hiding in her sewing room vanished as her feet carried her to the door. When she opened it, she discovered three young women crowded on the upper landing. One tall, one short and one with three narrow scars on her face. She recognized them from church.

Without a word, but holding her finger to her lips, she motioned for them to enter. All three women nodded, understanding her unspoken request to be quiet so Josie wasn't roused. She noticed one woman carried a box the perfect size for a pie, and another held a plastic bowl. She sighed. Waiting for her guests to finish the tea or *kaffi* she should serve along with what they'd brought could take more than an hour. By then, Josie would be stirring, ending any hopes Emma had of finishing the next-to-last shirt she had contracted for the rodeo participants.

"Hi, Emma. I'm Tyler's sister. Mollie," said the woman with the scarred cheek as she took off her bonnet, then her black wool coat. She draped them over the chair by the door.

Emma guessed Mollie was about her age. "I know who you are." She looked at the other women. "I know your names, too. Ruthanne, ain't so?"

The shortest woman, who looked to be close to Emma's age also, nodded, a strand of her dark hair falling over her brown eyes. She pushed it back with a motion as habitual as when Emma shoved her glasses up her nose.

"You're Carrie," Emma said.

The tall, blond woman smiled, her green eyes crinkling. She appeared to be several years younger than the others. She held a plastic bowl with a bright blue cover. "You're three for three."

"Two for two," Emma corrected before she could halt herself. "Mollie introduced herself, so I can't give my memory credit for that."

The three women chuckled, and she let her shoulders droop from their tightness. Instead of lamenting about the work not getting done, she should be grateful for callers. Coming to live in Lost River had changed her life, and she needed to embrace those changes.

And the man who made it possible? teased a soft voice deep in her mind.

Hushing the words only she'd heard, Emma invited the women to sit. There was room for two on the sofa, and she brought two chairs from the dining table.

Mollie held out the box. "Here you go."

"I'll get us *kaffi* to go with the pie," Emma began. "If—"

Smiling, Tyler's sister interrupted, "It's not pie. It's a taco-salad mix for your supper."

"Mollie is famous for her taco salad," Ruthanne said, grinning. "Word is she found her way into her husband's heart with taco salad."

"Then I'll be careful to whom I serve it," Emma said.

As they laughed together, she savored the

sound. She hadn't had close friends since her parents' deaths because, as she'd told Tyler, her *aenti* had lamented how difficult it was to abide with a single *kind* in her house. Having more would have been intolerable, so she'd refused to allow Emma to invite others or let her go to others' homes.

"If you accept their hospitality, you have to extend it," *Aenti* Pearl had insisted.

It hadn't made sense to Emma, but arguing could have incurred too big a risk. That she'd learned after the first time her *aenti*'s hand had left its imprint on her cheek.

"The ingredients in the bowl should be refrigerated," Mollie said while Carrie offered Emma the plastic bowl. "What's in the box can sit on the counter. If you don't want it tonight, it can go in the fridge. I've put cooking instructions inside."

"You're kind. *Danki*." Emma took the box and bowl. Carrying them into the kitchen, she added over her shoulder, "Can I get you a cup of something warm though we don't have pie?"

Ruthanne shook her head. "We can't stay because we know you're busy this time of day. We wanted to bring you an apartment-warming meal."

"That's kind of you."

"It's something we should have done a long time ago," Mollie said. "We should have welcomed you when you first arrived in the valley.

All I can say is we're glad we've had the opportunity to visit today."

"We've heard how much you like to sew," Ruthanne said before Emma could reply. "That you're making fancy clothes for *Englischers*."

"*Ja*. Would you like to see?"

Eagerness blossomed in each woman's eyes as Carrie said, "We'd love to."

After putting the bowl in the refrigerator and the box on the counter, Emma led the way into her workroom. The women were intrigued with her sewing machine and the embroidery on the shirts she'd already finished. When she explained she used her sewing machine to do the embroidery, they pelted her with questions.

"Tyler was right when he told me you had skills I'd love to learn," Mollie said, then chuckled. "'Tyler was right.' I haven't said those words many times. You know how it is with brothers and sisters."

The other two women nodded with wry expressions, but Emma said, "I was an only *kind*."

"All the more reason," Ruthanne announced, "why we should have invited you to join us sewing sisters before now."

"What are sewing sisters?"

"It's the name we've given our quilting group," Carrie replied. "We meet at each other's houses. There are about a half dozen of us, but it's seldom everyone can be there each week. We're sisters of the needle and thread, connected through our love of needlework." She looked at the main room, appraising it. "Do you quilt?"

"No," Emma said. "I've finished a few tops on my sewing machine. I appreciate your invitation, but—"

Carrie interrupted her. "Before you say no, I've got an idea if it's okay with you."

"That you have an idea?" Emma asked. "Ideas are fine with me."

Laughing before she answered, Carrie said, "I'll try again." She held up her finger to reinforce her pause. "If it's okay with you, Emma, we could bring our sewing when it's your turn to be the hostess. There's always mending to take care of. When you come to one of our houses, you can join us quilting. We'll teach you what we do if you teach us about what you do."

"That's a brilliant idea." Mollie grinned. "Do say *ja*. We're casual, Emma, and we talk and quilt and eat whatever someone's brought to share."

"You eat as you quilt?" Emma couldn't halt herself from looking at her hands. No scars were visible, but she hadn't ever forgotten the slash of *Aenti* Pearl's ruler across her fingers when Emma made the mistake of finishing a cookie at her sewing machine. There had been a single crumb—not even on the fabric—but her *aenti* had punished her as if Emma had dumped grape juice onto expensive silk. The ruler had broken,

and Emma had feared at least one bone in her
hand had been broken as well. The pain had been
horrendous for weeks, but she hadn't asked to see
a *doktor*. Her *aenti* wouldn't have agreed to pay
for an office visit.

"Especially when Mollie's *mamm* sends something with her." Ruthanne smiled at her friend.
"Dolly Yarwood is a *gut* cook, but her *mamm*
is the best baker in the whole valley. Maybe the
whole state."

"The whole world," Carrie added. "Wait until
you taste her glazed doughnuts. You'll never want
to eat anyone else's ever again!"

"That sounds like fun." As she spoke the simple words, Emma struggled to remember the last
time she'd done anything with women her age
that she could have described as fun. She hadn't
realized how much she needed friends.

She wouldn't forget again.

Chapter Seven

Emma frowned at her sewing machine as she heard Josie waking up in the other room. The needle kept catching the fabric. Only Emma's quick actions had kept the cotton pieces from being ruined. She would have to check the needle, the bobbin and the rest of the machine, but now was time to spend with Josie and give her eyes a rest. Pushing her chair back from the machine, she rubbed her eyes and her forehead. Her eyes were dry, and her head ached to her shoulders. Stress, she knew, but she had a *gut* reason when her reliable machine wasn't working.

At least she'd finished the rodeo shirts. The white-and-red gingham checked shirts hung on her low rolling rack. Her hard work had paid off. Or so she hoped. She'd be delivering them to an address on the other side of Lost River tomorrow. Mrs. Rose, who'd hired her, had requested Emma hold on to the shirts until her husband and son returned from a rodeo in Florida. Emma hadn't known there were rodeos that far east, but Mrs.

Rose told her there were several each year in the Sunshine State alone. The two were supposed to arrive home late tonight, so Emma would deliver the shirts tomorrow after Josie's nap.

She went into the bedroom, where Josie was standing in her crib and bouncing with excitement. What a blessed gift from God the *boppli* was! Her enthusiasm dissipated Emma's low thoughts. How could anyone be miserable when the little girl was happy?

A quick change and Josie was ready for playtime while Emma tried to decide what to have for supper. She smiled broadly when she remembered Mollie had brought the taco salad earlier. All she had to do was warm it up, put the ingredients together and eat. That would allow her time after supper to determine what was wrong with her sewing machine.

Footfalls on the interior steps came toward her apartment. It had to be Tyler. Did he have news about Gil? He'd promised Emma he'd share updates on Gil as soon as he got them from Dolly. The stairs gave a now familiar creak before Emma opened the door. On the other side, Tyler stood in the light from the bare bulb overhead. It emphasized the blond streaks in his hair, making them as bright as his smile.

"*Komm* in," she said.

"*Danki*." His smile broadened when Josie crawled toward him. The little girl paused by the sofa and pulled herself up. Gripping the cushion with tiny fingers, she waved her other hand toward him.

"Die, Die, Die!" she said, babbling.

"I hope that's not an order," he said, glancing at Emma.

"That's her way of saying your name." She laughed. "'Die' for 'Ty.' She can't manage the second syllable of your name yet."

He took the *boppli*'s hand and kept her upright while she took a couple of unsteady steps toward him. When she was about to tumble, he lifted her to his chest. She patted his shirt and repeated, "Die, Die, Die."

"Josie, Josie, Josie," he said to her, earning another grin.

"Dem, Dem, Dem." She pointed at Emma.

His brow furrowed as he said, "She doesn't call you *mamm*?"

"No. Why would she? I'm not her *mamm*. Sharon is."

Tyler was startled at Emma's genuine amazement. Searching his memories of her and the *boppli*, he was shocked to realize that he'd never heard Josie call her *mamm*.

"What does she say when she wants you? *Aenti* Emma?" The wrong question, he realized, when Emma shuddered. Again, he wondered why the mere mention of the word *aenti* distressed her.

He almost asked, then reminded himself he had things he didn't want to discuss with anyone else.

"She calls me 'Dem.'" She smiled as she gathered Josie to her after the little girl put out her hands in a silent request. "Sometimes it's 'Demma' when I don't answer her straightaway." Without a pause, she asked, "Do you need my help downstairs?"

"Not right now. I came up to let you know that Dolly called."

"How's Gil doing?"

"Much better. He's coming home tomorrow instead of staying at the rehab hospital."

"That's *wunderbaar*…and not *wunderbaar*. On one hand, it'll be simpler when Dolly doesn't have to drive to Lake City and back. He'll recover much better at home. However, Dolly is going to be stretched thin between the shop and being home for him."

He nodded, grateful for Emma's clear insight. "I'll be there tomorrow morning when they get home. She's not sure she can get him inside because there are two steps up to their porch and another into the house."

"I'll work downstairs while you're over there. That way, if something is delivered, I can sign for it."

"*Danki*. In addition, Dolly is wondering if you'd continue to work until she can get back full-time. She hopes that'll be by the beginning of next week."

"*Ja*, for as long as she needs me."

"I thought you'd say that."

"So you told her already I would."

He raised his palms skyward and shrugged. "Guilty as charged. I know it's not right to assume, but I figured this was a no-brainer."

"You assumed right, but I'll need time to work on my sewing."

"I realize that. A couple of hours in the morning will be all I need most of the time."

"Most of the time?" She put Josie on the floor and stepped aside as the *boppli* crawled to the sofa and began to pull herself up again.

"We've got two more orders to be delivered. I'll need your help with inventory again. That may take more than the morning."

She glanced toward her sewing room, and his gaze followed hers. From where he stood, he could see a jumbled collection of vibrant fabrics stacked on the table beside her sewing machine. Were those the square-dancing costumes she was making for Dolly and Gil?

Before he could ask, she faced him. Had she moved toward him or had he inched toward her? Or had it been mutual? They stood so close she couldn't have held the *boppli* between them. His fingers quivered as he fought to keep them from rising to brush a strand of bright red hair from her cheeks, which were the soft pink of snow burnished by the sunset. Was her skin as cool as the snow, or warm as if the sun was caressing it now? He longed to caress her face, cup her chin and...

He backed away before he could give in to his yearning to touch her. Had he lost every bit of sense he'd ever had? She was a plain woman. Though his *Englisch* friends talked of flirting with women and kissing them, he knew, for an Amish woman, such actions could mean more than just carefree fun.

Hearing her soft steps behind him, he imagined how it would be if she put her arms around him. He would turn, and draw her to him as his mouth found hers.

"Dem! Dem!" called Josie, and the moment vanished, along with his foolish hopes.

Emma picked up a book off the sofa before Josie could get her little hands on it. The title on the cover was something about a square-dancing conference and sewing tips for costumes, but he couldn't see more before she put it on the dining-room table out of Josie's reach.

He had to wonder if she'd used the book as an excuse to edge away from him. Because she suspected he was about to do something *dumm*, or because she thought she might? That yearning overwhelmed him again.

Emma said, "Your sister and her friends

stopped by earlier this afternoon. Do I have you to thank for their call, Tyler?"

He took a slow breath to steady his voice. "Mollie asked me how you and Josie were settling in. I may have said she should check for herself." He laughed but it sounded feigned to his ears. "One thing you need to know about my family. They are what they call curious. Others might consider them nosy."

"Not like you, ain't so?"

"Most definitely not like me. I mind my own business."

She arched her eyebrows as she glanced around the apartment.

"Maybe I should have said I usually mind my own business." Her teasing was helping him to regain his composure. Was she doing that on purpose?

"Mollie, Ruthanne and Carrie invited me to join their quilt circle."

He heard her hesitancy. "Are you?"

"They told me they'd teach me about quilting if I'd teach them about machine embroidery."

"Sounds like a fair trade. Did you say *ja*?" He wasn't sure why it was important to him.

You know, chided his conscience. *You want her to put down roots in Lost River, though you don't know if you can.*

Tyler tried to ignore the silent voice, but he

smiled when Emma nodded. Everything might change if her cousin arrived to reclaim her *kind*, but his doubts had grown with each passing day that Sharon Miller would ever show her face in Lost River again. How would Emma react if another year and another after that passed, and Josie remained with her? Or worse, what would happen if years went by and *then* Sharon walked into Emma's life?

To cover up his unsettling thoughts, he said, "Mollie told me she was going to bring you one of her taco-salad mixes."

"She did." Giving him an uncertain smile, she asked, "Are you fishing for an invitation to supper?"

His stomach growled an answer before words could. "If so, I'm not doing it with much subtlety."

"Being subtle doesn't seem to be your style."

Chuckling, he said, "True. Are you going to invite me to stay for my sister's taco salad?"

"If you'll play with Josie, I'll heat up the beef and put everything together. I was about to do that when you came upstairs."

"That's the best offer I've had today." Sitting on the floor, he faced the little girl who regarded him seriously.

That changed when he picked up a stuffed cat and made it dance as he began to sing about

Old MacDonald's farm and his menagerie. She seemed to know the song because she began to try to sing the chorus, though her version was closer to "de-I-de-I-do."

A half hour later, as mouth-watering aromas filled the apartment and wind gusted against the windows, Emma put a steaming casserole dish on the table. She set the fixings and taco shells beside it. While she got *millich* from the refrigerator, Tyler drew the high chair to the table and put Josie in it. The *boppli* bopped the tray with her hands as she babbled what might have been a verse of "Old MacDonald" until Emma handed her a sippy cup. She set a glass in front of him.

"Millich?" asked Tyler. "Is this a warning you've added a lot of spice to the taco salad?"

"It might be." Dimples appeared on either side of her lips. "Mollie suggested I should add as much chili as I wanted, and since I moved here, I've learned that I like spicy food."

When she sat, he bowed his head along with her. He silently thanked God for the food, for Gil's homecoming and for Emma and Josie's company. He found himself repeating the last twice more. When he realized that, he cleared his throat and raised his head to put an end to the silent prayer. He was surprised when he saw Josie do the same. Emma was holding her hand.

"Have you already taught Josie to be quiet during grace?" he asked.

"Ja." She made a face at the *boppli*, who giggled. "She's a *gut* girl, ain't so?"

"Could you teach my nephew to sit still during grace?"

"How old is he?"

"Six."

She shook her head. "That's an impossible age not to fidget. Ask me again when he's eighteen."

"Still impossible." He smiled as she took his plate and began to spoon the steaming meat mixture into a pair of taco shells. "I didn't learn to sit still until a couple of years ago."

As she handed him his plate and motioned for him to serve himself from the bowl that held lettuce, tortilla strips and a variety of fresh chopped vegetables, she said, "Some people never learn."

She didn't add more, and he refrained from asking when she'd mastered the skill. That shadow had passed through her eyes again as it did each time there was a reference to her past. Was it as simple as she missed Indiana and wished she could return there, but didn't want to risk not reconnecting with her cousin? Or did that dimness have something to do with the mysterious *aenti* she avoided talking about?

Wanting to make her smile, he asked, "Did Ruthanne and Carrie tell you their theory that Mollie caught her husband's—Noah's—heart with her taco salad?"

Emma flushed, and he knew he'd found the source of her earlier trepidation. *"Ja."*

"You shouldn't listen to them." He picked up his fork and gave it a careless wave. "I know for a fact Mollie didn't capture Noah's heart with her taco salad. It was *Mamm*'s coconut-custard pie that did the trick."

Putting her hands up over her mouth, she tried to hide her grin. He wanted to tell her it was futile because her eyes danced with amusement. That humor was aimed at herself, he realized.

He took her hands and lowered them from her face. "You shouldn't try to hide what you're feeling. Let the world see. If they don't like it, it's their problem, not yours."

"Is that what you do?"

He was about to say *ja* when he realized it wasn't the truth. How much had he hidden from family and friends since *Daed* had gotten sick? He'd pretended to be carefree, and to be able to handle every challenge that came his way and put away his grief long before it was ready to let him go.

"I try." He took a big bite of his taco to keep from having to say more, then grasped his glass as heat detonated on his tongue. Panting, he gulped down the *millich*.

Emma jumped to her feet, rushed to the refrigerator and returned with the carton. She refilled his glass before sitting down. "I warned you."

"I know. I know." He gasped and took another drink. "I didn't guess you'd add enough chili to set off smoke alarms. Think how embarrassing it would be for my brother to show up with the rest of the fire department to put out the fire in my mouth."

"People might pay to see that."

He laughed and set his empty glass on the table. When she refilled it a second time, he asked if she'd have enough for Josie. She assured him she would, and they focused on their food until he asked her how her sewing was going.

Her shoulders tightened as her fingers did on her fork. He understood why when she explained what had happened before he came upstairs. When he offered to look at the machine, she nodded, grateful.

After they'd finished eating, Emma took the remaining food to the kitchen and stored it while Tyler lifted Josie out of her chair. The little girl called his name. He sat beside her and exclaimed over each of the toys she handed him. He opened a board book and began to read her a story about the animals on the thick pages. When she leaned her head against his arm, he was sure his heart had filled to overflowing.

Tyler kept his regretful sigh quiet when Emma picked up the *boppli* and sat with her on the sofa as Josie had her bedtime bottle. He didn't let it out until he walked into her sewing room. Spending time with the little girl was fun. Everything was new and interesting to her. How could he have thought he'd be bored by little ones?

As he checked Emma's sewing machine, he listened while she talked to Josie. The *boppli* replied in her unique language. Words were secondary, however. Love filled each thing they said.

What would happen when—if—Sharon returned? What would happen if she didn't? He wished that thought didn't burst into his head so often, but he couldn't push it aside. If Emma's cousin showed up in Lost River and wanted to take her daughter, Josie wouldn't understand being wrenched away from the only *mamm* she knew, and Emma, who wouldn't hesitate to do what she believed was the right thing in reuniting *mamm* and *kind*, would be shattered.

There had to be a solution, but as with his dilemma about how he wanted to spend his life, he couldn't see it.

Josie was half-asleep on Emma's lap when he came into the main room. Rain was pounding against the window, and he thought it might be hailing. A horrible night to drive home. Maybe he'd sleep downstairs or go over to the Yarwoods' house and use their couch.

"I didn't see anything wrong with the sewing machine," he said as he sat at the table. Probably better not to share the sofa.

"Maybe there's a burr on the needle. It's a new

one, but sometimes that happens. I'll check it to-morrow." She rocked the *boppli*. "After I deliver the shirts I've finished. I hope it's not still rain-ing. I need to deliver them to a section of town I haven't visited before."

"You haven't seen much of the valley, ain't so?"

"Only what we passed when we arrived, and that was a blur. We were tired from the long bus ride."

Just as you're tired now, he wanted to say, but didn't. She'd be offended if he suggested she couldn't handle taking care of Josie and her sew-ing and unpacking downstairs.

"The day after tomorrow," he said, "I'm head-ing to Crestline to pick up storage units Dolly ordered. Gil was supposed to go, but that's not going to happen now. Do you want to *komm* with me? Dolly thought it might be a nice outing for you and Josie."

"Crestline? Where's that?"

"It's north and west of here. Right up against the San Juan Mountains. It's about a ninety-min-ute drive."

Her eyes widened behind her glasses. "You're planning to drive? Plain folks don't—"

"I know, but I can drive because I'm not bap-tized." He wished he could stop feeling like a complete failure each time he admitted that. The simple solution, his family would have told him, was to take baptism preparation classes with the bishop.

Again.

How many times had he attended the sessions that ended with participants stepping forward to be baptized?

He knew. Twice. As well as a couple of more times, when he'd gone to a class or two before coming up with lame excuses why he couldn't go to the rest.

"Oh," she said.

When she didn't add anything else, he knew he should. Right away. Before the silence could claim them as if they were caught on flypaper, stuck and unable to move. He wasn't sure what else to say. How could he explain to Emma what he didn't understand himself?

"If you'd like to go," he said as he got up and walked toward the door to the interior stairs, "I'll be leaving about nine."

He wasn't sure what he dreaded more—her saying she wouldn't go, or that she would. Would she save him from his own foolishness by turning him down? A few weeks ago, he would have protested if anyone had suggested he'd let another woman slip into his thoughts and linger there. Now, he was eager to arrange opportunities for them to be together.

That was why his heart did a quick double-beat when she said, "*Ja*, that sounds like fun."

Fun? As he hurried down the stairs, he hoped she was right because he sensed that, one way or the other, this trip would change their relationship.

He just wasn't sure how.

Chapter Eight

When she heard a knock on the interior door, Emma didn't look up from the embroidery on the shirt she was making for Dolly. She didn't want to halt the line now, because it wasn't simple to realign the new zigzag needle to make the line smooth. The pattern was a pair of roses that would match the ones she intended to put on the wide, ruffled skirt.

"Hi, Dolly," she called from her sewing room, glad Josie had already finished her nap and was playing on the floor.

"I'm not Dolly." Tyler stuck his head around the door.

Her heart did an excited leap, but she made sure she'd put the needle in the fabric before she pushed back her chair. "Tyler! I didn't expect to see you."

"I didn't expect to be here." He pointed toward the stairs. "Gil can't get up here for his fitting. I've been sent in his place."

Her brow ruffled with confusion. "You're doing a fitting for Gil?"

"Dolly says we're close in size and you're a *gut* enough seamstress so it shouldn't matter."

Emma couldn't resist rolling her eyes. "I don't agree, though I know she meant that as a compliment."

"For you or for me?"

She couldn't restrain her laugh. When Josie looked at her and began to jabber, she stood before bending to pick up the *boppli*. "See? Josie thinks it's silly."

"That makes three of us. I didn't plan to spend the day as a mannequin."

"As a dress form."

He rested his shoulder against the doorframe. "What's a dress form?"

She put one hand on the fabric-covered torso beside her sewing machine. "This."

"It's got no legs or arms."

"And no head."

"I hope that's not how Dolly sees me." He made a face that sent Josie into peals of giggles.

"No, she's glad you have arms and legs to tote things around and put them in their proper places."

He grimaced at her. "*Danki*… I think."

"You're welcome… I think." After propping Josie on her hip, she picked up a collection of fabric pieces from the table. She set them on the sewing machine, far enough away from Dolly's shirt so she didn't jostle the half-finished rose petal.

"What's that?" Tyler asked.

"A square-dancing shirt for Gil. In pieces." She sat Josie on the blanket again. "Stand in the middle of the room, and I'll pin it to see if it's going to fit." When he reached for the top button on his shirt, she said, "You can put it on right over your clothes."

"Are you sure you can get proper measurements?"

"Close enough, and this way I shouldn't prick you as I pin it."

"*Danki* for the warning."

Emma wrapped his humor around her as she drew out a small stool from the corner. Stepping on it, she draped the two pieces of yoke that would go over his shoulders. She pinned the sleeves on.

"Don't move," she cautioned as she edged around him. "Gil's arms are wider than yours, so this should be a *gut* approximation."

"I've got skinny arms? Is that what you're telling me?"

"No! That's not what I meant. Your arms are fine," she replied before his crinkling eyes warned he'd been teasing her.

"I'm glad you think so."

Suddenly she felt exposed when she stood close

to him. Telling herself to act as if she pinned shirts onto the muscular arms of handsome men every day, she said aloud, "Maybe you shouldn't talk, Tyler."

"Because I'm shifting the pieces?"

"No, because I might jab you to stop your nonsense."

He started to laugh, then froze when the fabric started to fall off his shoulders. "Sorry," he said, squeezing out the word between tight lips.

Emma relented, glad she could jest with him when she was finding it tough to draw in a steady breath. "Go ahead and talk. It's okay." It'd be better than okay because whatever he said was certain to take her mind off how appealing he smelled and how his arms, above her shoulders, could settle on them in an embrace.

You shouldn't be having such thoughts.

Chiding her brain was useless. She was *ab in kopp*—out of her mind!—if she let her thoughts loiter on Tyler. If he'd wanted a wife, he could have had his choice among the *maedels*. None of whom was raising a *boppli* that wasn't their own.

Again, her mind argued with her. Josie *was* hers. Maybe Emma hadn't given birth to Josie, but she'd made her the center of her life for the past year.

She told herself to stop being silly. About Josie and about Tyler. Instead, she asked about Gil, as she should have right at the beginning, and listened while she finished pinning the shirt. When she was done, she had Tyler bend so she could lift it over his head. She thanked God when she got it off him without a single pin scratching him.

She put it on the table, then smoothed it out, noting where the pieces didn't fit together as she'd hoped. The shoulders weren't abutting the top of the sleeves, but she wouldn't sew insets in until she confirmed the fitting on Gil.

"Do you have enough fabric for the spots where it doesn't match up?" Tyler asked as he looked at the shirt.

"I've got plenty."

"How will you fit it together with odd pieces? Won't it look strange?"

"I can fix any spots with embroidery. It seems to go against logic, but people won't notice a mistake if it's decorated."

He turned toward her sewing machine. "Is that what you're doing there? Covering up a mistake?"

"No. That embroidery is intentional. I'm putting a rose on Dolly's shirt."

"I thought embroidery was done with a hoop and a needle."

"I use both, but with a zigzag machine." After putting Josie on the floor, where she could keep an eye on the *boppli*, she sat at her machine again. "Let me show you."

Tyler stood behind her, and she was aware of his breath on her nape beneath her *kapp* when he leaned forward to see her work. She gripped her apron, then forced her fingers to relax. If they shook when she worked, she could ruin what she'd already done.

"You put the hoop on your sewing machine," he said, each word an individual caress along the top of her dress. "Isn't it difficult to get a hoop under the needle?"

"It's a special kind of hoop. Wood instead of plastic, like most hoops are now. Also, it's not as tall, and it's got a screw to tighten it rather than pushing the two hoop pieces together. That way, I can adjust the fabric to the proper tension, which has to be firm."

"You might as well be speaking Latin." He squatted so his eyes were level with the needle. "You're going to have to demonstrate."

"Okay." She put her foot on the controller on the floor and eased it down to start the needle.

"You forgot to put the foot down!"

Emma smiled. "You, Tyler Lehman, know more about sewing than you've let on."

"I know from watching *Mamm* make our clothes that you've got to put the foot thingy down on the fabric to hold the material in place while the needle goes up and down."

"Not when I'm embroidering. I leave the foot up, and I've lowered the feed dogs. The little plates with tiny teeth beneath the needle that moves the fabric. The fabric needs to go where I want it to, not just forward."

Again, she started the machine. Making herself focus on what she was doing rather than Tyler, she used the needle to outline the rest of the rose petal. Neither of them spoke as the bright red zigzag thread filled in the pattern to create a rose.

Emma lifted the needle out of the fabric and cut the threads from above and the bobbin below. Turning over the yoke, she showed him how she used white thread to conceal the pattern on the underside of the shirt.

"That's amazing," he said, pushing himself to his feet. "Did your *aenti* teach you to do this embroidery?"

The warmth that had delighted her when he was close vanished into the all-too-familiar icy void where she'd dwelled for the majority of her life. "I first learned from *Mamm*."

Surprise flashed across his face. "I've never heard you talk about your *mamm* before."

"I don't have many memories of her and my *daed*."

"I'm sorry, Emma."

"Why? You didn't know them." She hated the bitterness in her voice, but it reemerged each time anyone invoked her past. Standing, she edged away from him.

"I know you. You're a *gut*, caring person, so they must have been, too. If I were to imagine how lost Josie would be if something happened to you, I know how lost you must have felt when your parents died."

Her breath caught, and the protective barricades she'd kept between her and the pain of the past began to waver. His kind tone, as if he comprehended what she'd withstood, was undermining them as nothing and nobody ever had. She wanted to escape before her defenses failed. At the same time, she longed to run into his arms so she could find healing by connecting with someone who cared about her.

She didn't. She'd believed others cared for her, but each had left her. She wasn't going to make that same stupid mistake again.

Tyler slowed the rusty black pickup as he reached the first houses at the edge of tiny Crestline. It wasn't big enough to be called a town. Like many of the small settlements beneath the sharp peaks of the San Juan Mountains, it'd first been established as a mining town. Miners had rushed through the San Luis Valley or traveled north from what was now New Mexico and had spent months or years seeking their fortunes. Few had succeeded, and most had left as quickly as they'd arrived, following rumors of the next big strike.

Dolly and Gil knew he liked visiting the town. He guessed that's why they'd asked him to pick up the storage units instead of hiring a delivery service. He loved the mountains, even when they weren't covered with snow. Something about them made his heart want to lift and soar on the thermals like a hawk over the undulating peaks.

His favorite skiing spot was the Bison Springs Resort on the far side of these mountains. There, he could throw aside his problems while he skied down the mountain or across a ridge or around giant boulders. He had to remain on alert for dangers the mountain might have lying in wait for him.

And he had to do the same with Emma. Each time he thought she'd open up about her past, she slammed the door closed and twisted locks around those memories. No, not locks, because what had happened to her continued to have a stranglehold on her. The vibrant, enticing woman she could have been was overshadowed by grief and the fear that she'd never measure up to others' expectations.

He wanted to tell her the only expectations she had to meet were God's and her own, but how could he? He was fighting a similar battle.

Beside him, Emma moved, pulling his attention to the present. She'd been checking on Josie in her car seat, but her gaze was now aimed out the windshield, as his was.

"Wow!" she murmured.

"Yeah." He chuckled at her awe. Not that he

faulted her. The mountains rising around them were spectacular. *Raw* was how he'd heard them described, but to him they looked like a project God had started and was taking His time to complete to His satisfaction, though Tyler couldn't imagine how the view could have been improved. "The mountains are pretty amazing, ain't so?"

"It looks like a giant put down a huge serrated knife on its side with the top of each point concealed beneath snow."

He had to chuckle at her fanciful description. "I never thought of it like that, but you're right. A serrated knife with trees growing out of it."

"There are patches where nothing is growing."

"Those spots are where there were landslides or avalanches in the past. The falling stone or snow rips the trees right out of the ground. At the bases of those peaks, you can see boulders as big as a house. They tumbled down maybe a hundred years ago. Maybe last week. The mountains are recreating themselves."

"As if God has His eye on them."

He smiled, then glanced out the side window. "I should warn you Crestline is different," he said as they passed a full-size tepee that hadn't been there the last time he'd visited a few months ago. Now, laundry flapped in the breeze on a clothesline. A satellite dish had been set up next it. A happy face and a peace sign were outlined in

Day-Glo orange on the tent. "Crestline collects people who don't fit in anywhere else."

"What do you mean?"

"First it was miners and homesteaders. Lately it's been massage therapists and old hippies."

She smiled, and the interior of the truck seemed to heat a few pleasant degrees. "Old hippies?"

"You know the type of people I mean."

"No, not really. I never met anyone in Indiana who called themselves 'an old hippie.'"

"Welcome to Colorado. All sorts come here to find a separate life in the mountains and among the valleys."

"Sounds familiar," she said with a smile.

"The people who have settled in Crestline dropped out in the 1960s and 70s and never dropped back in. They want to find simple lives disconnected to the grid, and they're dependent on their hard work to sustain them."

"Sounds familiar."

He had to laugh. "*Ja*, I guess it does, but these folks aren't Amish. Though most are peace-loving and accepting of people who aren't like themselves."

"Again, sounds familiar."

"I never looked at Crestline that way." He chuckled again. "Maybe that's why I like the place. That or the homemade ice cream at the convenience store in the center of town."

He turned the truck right at the first corner

and continued along the main thoroughfare. The road was barely wide enough for two vehicles, and it became hard-packed dirt. Clouds of dust announced every vehicle. Pedestrians swatted the dust aside.

Tyler edged to the right to let a car towing a gigantic RV past them. The other vehicle's right wheels bounced onto the narrow sidewalk to splash through a few slushy puddles. Nobody seemed to mind as they jumped onto porches or paused between buildings to let the RV pass with more dust and a crunching sound each time one of the wheels dropped into a pothole.

"Look!" cried Emma. "It's a deer!"

Tyler stared, amazed when the animal didn't bound away. Instead, it walked across the dirt road through the dust cloud, glancing in their direction without curiosity. In the shade cast by a scraggly tree, the buck kneeled in the grass. It didn't stir when a dog barked at a house farther up the road.

"Let's let him take his nap," Emma said.

"It looks as if someone already had that idea." He smiled in the rearview mirror, which gave a *gut* angle to see Josie was asleep in her car seat.

"Where are we going?"

"Around the next corner." He turned onto a road that led between several more buildings. One was lime-green, another pink, while the other two were painted light brown. "So what do you think of Crestline?"

No other cars moved along the street, though there were several parked in front of a post office and a bank. The shops had doors decorated with crystals or painted stones or mirrors.

Emma's head swiveled as she tried to take in a Victorian house with two turrets across the street from a pyramid made from what looked like pallets nailed over logs. When they passed a metal sculpture of a gigantic ladybug, she laughed. "I've never seen anything like this place."

"Probably because there isn't any other place like Crestline."

"*Danki* for inviting me. I'm not sure I would have believed it if I didn't see it myself." She pointed to another building and gasped, "Look at that one. It's shaped like an elephant." She smiled. "Maybe I don't believe what I'm seeing with my own eyes."

He chuckled, realizing why making Emma smile brought him a pulse of happiness. She smiled often, but he could sense she was doing it because she believed it was the right thing to do, not because she felt like smiling. Much of what Emma did was aimed at making other people feel *gut* about themselves. Even when she didn't herself.

"Ah, here we are." Tyler turned off the dirt road and into a parking lot filled with construction materials. On the far side of the parking lot was a low-slung building. It looked like a cross between a garage and a circus tent, because striped canvas enclosed the front end of it where an artists' co-op claimed space that once had been a welding shop. He stopped the truck and opened his door. "Do you want to *komm* in?"

She looked over her shoulder at the sleeping *boppli.* "How long will you be?"

"About five minutes. Maybe less." Seeing a man emerge from a door about halfway along the building, he added, "There's Jeremy Dodds. He's the guy who's built the units for Dolly."

"It'd be better," Emma said, "if we stay where we're not in the way."

He heard a hint of remorse in her voice and wondered how often she'd been told to stay out of the way. Had it been her *aenti* or someone else? Dolly had warned him—more than once—to tread carefully if he broached the subject of Emma's life before she came to Lost River. Anyone could see she hadn't had an easy time.

If she trusted him, she might tell him about her past. Would that ever happen?

Tyler didn't have time to dwell on his thoughts as Jeremy, who was tall, skinny and without a hair on his head except for a luxuriant black beard, greeted him with a quick handshake. Jeremy was also a backcountry skier, and whenever Tyler came to Crestline, they spent an hour or two talking about their most recent adventures. That wouldn't be possible today.

Jeremy shot a glance over his shoulder as Tyler walked with him toward his workshop at the rear of the long building. "Company today?"

"A friend."

Jeremy grinned. "A good friend?"

"A friend."

Bending to peer past the reflection on the windshield, he said, "She's not bad on the eyes, Tyler. Sure she's not more than a friend?"

"*Ja.*" A pinch of something unnerving resonated out of his terse answer. Why? Because he'd like Emma to be more than a friend? Until he committed to baptism, he couldn't treat any woman as more than a casual acquaintance. Yet…

Jeremy poked him with an elbow. "Got someone on your mind?"

"Huh?"

"I asked what you thought of the display cases, and you stood there like a newbie visiting the mountains for the first time."

"Truth is, I do have someone on my mind. You heard Gil fell off his bike and messed himself up pretty bad, ain't so?" That wasn't a lie, though his thoughts had been focused on Emma, because he had been shocked yesterday to see how unsteady Gil still was on his crutches and how much pain his friend was in. The image of Gil's gray face had stayed with him since.

Jeremy hadn't heard about Gil's fall and pelted Tyler with questions. Tyler answered them as much as he could. As he walked deeper into the building with the carpenter, he resisted the urge to check if Emma and Josie were all right. It had to be for the best if he and Emma didn't become dependent on each other in any way. Who knew how long she'd stay in Lost River if Sharon came to reclaim her daughter? Or how long he'd stay if he decided to accept a job with the ski patrol? Remaining friends and nothing more, as he'd described them to Jeremy, would be the smart thing.

So why was his heart telling him he was stupid to have such thoughts?

Chapter Nine

Tyler was gone for five minutes, and then fifteen more. Emma considered a couple of times getting Josie out of the truck and going to discover what was delaying him. She told herself patience was a virtue she should learn to practice more often. Then Josie began to whimper, wanting to escape from her safety seat. Though it was cool outside and the window was rolled down, the little girl was sweating.

Emma slid out and unhooked the straps on Josie's safety seat. Josie threw herself in Emma's arms. Balancing the little girl on her hip, Emma walked around the truck several times, taking in the view of the fantastical buildings and the impressive mountains. She admired how the peaks glistened in the sunlight. For the first time, she could understand why miners had swarmed over them in search of gold and silver and other treasures. Though one part of her mind knew the glitter came from the wet faces of the crags, where snow was melting, another couldn't help imagining nuggets of precious metals were embedded in the stone.

When Josie began to suck on her knuckles, Emma got a teething biscuit from the diaper bag and handed it to her. She stepped aside when Tyler and another man emerged from the building. They carried a glass-fronted display case, which they slid into the pickup.

"We'll get the other one right away," Tyler said, wiping his hands on his black trousers as the other man strode toward the building. "A door latch was broken on this one, and Jeremy had to replace it."

"You don't need to explain. We were admiring the view."

"*Gut*. Look. Here comes our friend the deer."

"It's a doe, not the buck we saw before." Emma held her breath as the deer walked past them as if they weren't there. "She looks tame enough that we could go over and pet her."

The doe paused by a small creek that trickled past the parking lot. On the other side stood a log cabin decorated with devices to catch the wind. They created flashes of color and an endless variety of notes, with metallic and plastic and wooden tones.

"I wonder how those folks sleep on a windy night," Tyler said.

"Probably like a *boppli* being sung a lullaby."

A dull thump resonated through the afternoon. The deer froze, her gaze darting in every direction.

Emma realized she'd had an identical reaction. She scanned the yard between the house and the creek. A thick pine that had a large board attached to it swayed in the breeze. When the plywood came around enough, it struck a mallet, sending another thud toward them.

"*That* doesn't sound like a lullaby," Tyler said with a laugh.

"No, it sounds more like a *boppli*'s tummy when she has colic."

"Like I warned you, people in Crestline have plenty of odd ideas."

"I can see that." She was about to add more when the doe leaped over the creek in a single smooth motion.

The deer walked to a pine tree where the lowest branches were more than five feet from the ground. As easily as she'd jumped the creek, the doe rose on her hind feet and nibbled at the needles. Josie clapped her hands with excitement as the deer pulled at the branch, making it bounce and spill needles to the ground.

While it lapped up its feast, Tyler said, "Watching her makes me hungry. How about lunch before we leave?" He pointed to a tiny grocery store across the road. It was a low, stucco building with the word *Groceries* hand-painted over the door. "We can grab something there."

"Is that the place where they have homemade ice cream?" she asked.

"*Ja*, and they've got a new bakery. We can get something to eat before we head home. How does that sound?"

"Delicious! I'll get Josie's stroller set up."

"*Gut*. Let us get this other unit loaded on, and we'll be set."

"Are you leaving the truck?"

"Can I keep the truck in the parking lot, Jeremy?" he called to the other man, who'd paused in the doorway.

Jeremy walked back to them. "Pull your truck off to the side, and it shouldn't be in anyone's way. If it is, they'll work around it."

Emma shared a quick smile with Tyler before he followed Jeremy into the building. The men came out carrying an identical display case, which fit next to the first with a little maneuvering in the truck bed.

Jeremy wiped his hand across his nape. "Tell Dolly if she's got any questions or concerns to let me know." He grinned. "I know she will. She likes everything as she likes it."

"Who doesn't?" Emma asked before she could help herself.

The man chuckled as Tyler said, "Jeremy

Dodds, this is my friend Emma Weaver and her... and Josie."

Had Jeremy caught the hesitation in Tyler's voice? Emma didn't see any sign of it as the carpenter said, "Nice to meet you, Emma." He wiggled his fingers close to the *boppli*'s face, earning him a giggle. Straightening, he said, "Dolly is a perfectionist, but I don't have a problem with that. I am, too." He clapped Tyler on the shoulder. "And you. How many times did you try to ski from that high ridge on Bonanza Mountain until you made it? This guy is a beast on skis!" He slapped Tyler on the back again. "Takes risks none of the rest of us would dare to."

"He's exaggerating," Tyler said, but his easy grin had returned.

As she listened to the two men tease each other and talk about their ski adventures, Emma saw how comfortable Tyler was with an *Englischer*. She'd seen him interact often with the Yarwoods, but witnessing his carefree interaction with Jeremy made her own words replay through her mind.

Have you asked yourself if you're more comfortable among the Englisch *or among plain folk?*

He hadn't had an answer, and now she understood why. She sent up a quick prayer for God to help guide him.

Her thoughts were interrupted when Tyler

asked, "Ready for lunch?" He closed the rear of the truck and waved as the other man walked away.

"Are you set?" Emma asked.

"Ja." He reached over the side of the truck and tucked a moving blanket beneath the edge of the cabinet. "Dolly has been waiting for these two units for the storage she needs out front."

"What about the cabinets that are there now?"

"They're going in the back as soon as the kitchen equipment is moved out."

Her eyes widened. "I didn't realize there were appliances left in the store."

"Those are gone, but bowls and pans and other tools are packed in boxes." He leaned an elbow on the side of the truck's bed as he arched his eyebrows. "Don't feel bad you didn't notice. One cardboard box looks the same as any other."

He continued to tease her and Josie as they crossed the road to the tiny convenience store. They went to a tiny deli tucked in the front corner. Emma ordered a tuna salad for herself and toast for Josie. The little girl delighted in picking tiny pieces off a quarter slice of bread while Tyler waited for his roast-beef club. Some went in Josie's mouth, but more went onto her lap.

"She's enjoying herself," Tyler said at the small table near the front door where they'd settled themselves. They were out of the way of other customers and protected from dust that seeped around the door each time a vehicle passed.

"I hope they've got a broom I can use." Emma herded pieces of toast together with her foot. She took another bite of her delicious sandwich, delighted to discover kernels of sweet corn along with bits of celery and onion in the tuna salad.

Josie held out a smidgen of toast to Tyler. Pretending he was going to eat her fingers along with the toast, he grinned when she giggled and said, "Die! Die!"

Customers cast sideways glances at them, and Emma smiled. Explaining over and over what Josie meant to say would be silly. Instead, she enjoyed her sandwich and Tyler's clowning with the *boppli*.

A sense of contentment washed over her. When was the last time she'd felt such ease? That she was in the right place at the right time? Though it might be a fleeting illusion, she wanted to hold on to it. She'd spent years waiting for unhappiness to be replaced by joy, only to see her hopes dashed each time. Now, God had brought her to this unexpected moment in her life, and she was grateful.

"Ready for ice cream?" Tyler asked.

She looked down, discovering she'd finished every crumb of her sandwich while lost in thought. Raising her eyes, she locked her gaze with his compelling one. A myriad of emotions ricocheted through his eyes. She longed to sample each one, savor them and stitch them to her heart.

"Emma?"

Blinking as if awakening from a dream, she managed to smile. "I'm always ready for ice cream."

"I knew there was a reason I like you." He came to his feet before her gasp at his bold words could erupt out of her.

Emma bent down to the *boppli* again as if nothing was more important than brushing the crumbs off Josie's dress. After sweeping them onto her palm, she dumped them into the trash can. She had her face composed by the time she faced Tyler again, but her heart roiled with turbulent emotions. She'd hardened herself to ignore words. *Aenti* Pearl's complaints and scolds would have destroyed her if she hadn't inured her heart to them. *Onkel* Conrad's gentler words, which were never spoken when his wife might overhear, had done nothing to heal the invisible wounds afflicted on her.

Letting Tyler lead the way along the short, narrow aisle, she pretended to be interested in what was displayed on the shelves. She couldn't have said if there were boxes of cereal or rice or nails, because she was trying to sort out her conflicting feelings.

"Ice cream or doughnuts or both?" asked Tyler when he stopped at the rear of the store.

Instead of answering, Emma pushed the stroller around him so she could see the back counter. It held a selection of bread and cookies on one side next to a freezer case with large containers of ice cream. A fancy *kaffi* machine sat on a wide shelf behind where two women were restocking a tray of glazed doughnuts with a sign that read, *Help Yourself. One Per Customer, Please.*

She looked up at the menu board. "The Stottlemyer Bakery? That's a Mennonite name. Is this a plain bakery? In the San Juans?"

"Could be. There's a Mennonite bakery to the east of the Sangre de Cristo Mountains on the other side of the valley. In Westcliffe."

"Amish live there, too, ain't so?"

"Ja." He tapped his finger on his cheek. "Ice cream or doughnuts. What a tough choice!"

"Not tough at all," a blond woman who was behind the counter said. Her pale hair wasn't covered by any sort of *kapp*, not even the round doily type that more liberal Mennonite women wore. "Doughnuts are free for our customers. If you want a doughnut, we ask you to order something. Coffee or a tea or maybe ice cream." She gave a feigned shiver. "Though it's not ice-cream weather until the last of the snow is gone."

"What do you want, Emma?" he asked.

"Josie and I will share a glazed doughnut, and I'd like a green tea."

"Coming right up," the blonde replied as she

told Emma to take a doughnut. "How about you, sir?"

"A doughnut, but I'll have a chocolate *millich*... I mean, chocolate milk latte."

"Help yourself, sir, to a doughnut." The barista gave him a flirtatious smile, then looked at the stroller, where Josie was having her first taste of the doughnut. "I can see someone fancies our doughnut samples."

Josie smiled, her newest tooth on display between her cheeks, which were spotted with sugar and bits of dough.

The woman turned to make their drinks after giving Tyler another smile.

Tyler seemed impervious to her warm expression because he grabbed a couple of napkins and then picked up a doughnut. "Can't beat free."

"It's a brilliant sales tactic. Walk up to the display cases to get a free doughnut and walk out with something you pay for." She bent to offer another tiny piece of doughnut to Josie, who gobbled it with delight and held out her hands for more. The next bite the little girl squeezed between her fingers and chortled.

"Here." He held out another napkin.

"I'm going to need more than one to clean her up, but I'll wait until she's finished." She took a bite of the doughnut, enjoyed its sweetness on her tongue, then said, "I'll get our drinks. Will you take Josie up front? We can sit while we sip."

"Sounds like a plan." He reached for his wallet.

She put her hand out to halt him, then yanked her fingers away, half-expecting to see sparks darting between her skin and his. Somehow, she managed to keep her voice even. "You paid for lunch. Let me pay for this."

"Are you sure?"

"Absolutely." She made shooing motions with her hands, astonished she could act as if nothing had occurred when she touched him.

He nodded and took the stroller up the aisle. Had he failed to notice those flickers of sensation between them, or was he pretending, as she was?

Emma waited while the two women worked on their drinks, the scents of *kaffi* and sugar from the doughnuts permeating the air. When the barista stepped forward and put two cups on the counter, Emma said, "Are you a Stottlemyer?"

"I am. The name's a mouthful, isn't it?"

"Do you own the bakery?"

"My parents do. They opened a bakery in Pagosa Springs about fifteen years ago. They've spread out with five other shops, most small, like this one. As they have five kids, they've got plenty of help. I love Crestline, so I came here to work and paint." She gestured toward framed pictures on either side of the menu board. They depicted the mountains around the village.

"Stottlemyer is a Mennonite name, ain't so?"

"Our ancestors were Mennonite, but all we

have left are our surname and our love for baking." The woman grinned. "In fact, my great-grandparents were Amish. You're Amish, aren't you?"

"*Ja.*"

"I've always been curious how different my life would have been if my great-grandparents had remained Amish. They became Mennonite, and then somewhere along the way, we started going to a community church that suited us better." She rolled her eyes. "Sorry. I know you weren't asking for my family history."

"No, it's okay. Do you know why your great-grandparents left the Amish?"

The blonde shook her head. "I've heard stories. My grandfather said something about my great-grandfather wanting to take a job that his bishop… Is that right? Is a bishop the one who would have interfered with him taking his dream job?"

"Probably." The doughnut seemed to weigh a ton as it fell to the bottom of Emma's stomach along with her hopes.

"Anyhow, my great-grandfather and his family left the Amish, and they came to Colorado. On the eastern plains at first, but then into the mountains. I'm glad they did."

Emma managed to thank the woman before walking away. She didn't go far along the aisle before taking a shuddering breath. How many times had *Aenti* Pearl yelled at her for being fanciful and not seeing reality when Emma had wanted to join other girls her age at a youth event? Emma had been needed to work at home and make money to provide for her keep.

Don't fill your head with fairy tales. They don't come true. Aenti Pearl had repeated some variation of those words at least once a month from the time Emma had been deposited in her care.

Fool that she was, Emma had begun to believe her *aenti* was wrong after Sharon had left Josie with her. For the first time in many sad years, Emma had been able to thank God for the delight He'd brought into her life. She'd dared to have hopes, to have dreams, to accept that at last, with Josie, she had a family who wanted her.

Then Tyler had burst into her life. She'd told herself not to get involved, but hadn't resisted when he appeared again and again to brighten her days. She wasn't certain when eager anticipation of seeing him had evolved into the hope he'd be a part of her life forever. Why had she thought that when she'd seen, over and over, how easily he slipped into the *Englisch* world?

One thing she knew. If he decided to jump the fence like the barista's great-grandfather, he'd take her happiness with him.

Clouds chased the pickup to Lost River. When Tyler drove around to the rear of Mountain Sports and Adventures, he was grateful the rain had held off. Again, he wished he had his brother's ability to time the arrival of a storm. He left Emma to get the *boppli* out of the truck while he ran to get the wheeled dolly from the garage to move the storage cabinets inside the shop.

He wrestled the first one off the truck, tossing the moving blanket over the other when he felt the first drops of rain. The material wouldn't protect the wood long in a downpour.

"*Danki* for taking us with you," Emma said as she hurried toward the outside stairs.

Those had been the first words she'd spoken to him since they'd left Crestline. At first, he thought he'd said something to upset her. She hadn't regarded him with anger. Just fatigue and sadness. Though he'd wanted to probe what was bothering her, he didn't. Their day had been fun, and ruining the end of it would be *dumm*. Maybe she was tired. She'd been working hard on getting her sewing orders done, including the Yarwoods'. She'd helped him in the store and taken care of Josie without a break, other than the time each day when he played with the little girl while Emma made them lunch.

All thoughts except getting the two cabinets inside had to be pushed out of his head. There were three steps at the rear, so it'd be easier to get the cabinets inside from the front. He guided the first one around the building and onto the porch.

The glass rattled a warning when he unlocked the front door and pulled the storage cabinet over the threshold.

"You got them!" Dolly's joyful cry echoed through the dark store.

Shocked that someone was there, Tyler almost tipped the cabinet on its side. He wrapped his arm around the front to stabilize it before setting it upright.

"That's a fearsome expression," Dolly added.

Tyler looked up from checking the cabinet doors. Behind him, Dolly, dressed in bright colors, from the bow in her hair to the tips of her iridescent sneakers that appeared as if she'd stepped into a puddle topped with a smear of oil, had her hands at her waist and a smile pulling at her lips.

"You can't see my face," he retorted.

She laughed. "I don't need to. You jumped halfway to the roof when I spoke."

"Let me bring in the other cabinet before it gets drenched." He headed toward the front door, towing the dolly.

"I'll help."

"*Gut.* I'll have a dolly and a Dolly to bring it in."

When she grimaced, he motioned for her to hurry. As they rushed to the rear of the building through a thickening curtain of rain, he noticed lamps on upstairs. He was glad Emma and Josie were inside.

With Dolly's assistance, he kept a moving blanket wrapped around the cabinet while he got it out of the truck and into the store. Dolly updated him on Gil as they worked side by side.

"He can get around on his crutches pretty well if he doesn't go far," she said.

"Is he climbing the walls?"

Dolly chuckled. "To the ceiling. Gil isn't someone who likes to sit. He'd much rather be out on his bike, though it may take longer to repair his bike than his bones. He doesn't need me hanging around the house, so I figured I'd come to work so we still might be able to open the shop on time."

"We should be able to do that. Getting these cabinets was the last delivery we were waiting on." He began to slide the second cabinet into place.

She smiled. "Did you and Emma have fun in Crestline? It's an adorable place—the perfect place for you three to get away from hubbub in town."

"Stop it, Dolly!"

"Stop what?"

"I don't need you matchmaking." He shoved the table out of the way.

"Matchmaking? Me?"

He gave her a wry grin. "Don't act innocent. You suggested I take Emma—"

"And Josie."

"You suggested I take them with me, and you sent me upstairs for a fitting for Gil's shirt a couple of days ago."

Dolly gave him a quelling look. "I thought Emma would enjoy getting out of Lost River. She never goes anywhere. You've got to admit that's true."

"It is." He was starting to wonder why he'd opened his mouth.

"I sent you upstairs because Gil doesn't know how to avoid a pothole. For several days before his accident, I reminded him about his fitting with Emma. Did he remember? No. He went off to Pagosa Springs instead. Emma's been nice to take on the extra work for our square-dancing group. I'm not going to make it harder for her by having to go over to the house to do Gil's fittings because he couldn't hold on to his bike. You're close enough in size to him. I thought you'd be glad to help." She turned away and pushed the table toward the back room. "You've spent too much time with Gil. You're getting like him, seeing plots and conspiracies where there aren't any."

Taken aback, Tyler sought the best apology he could. "Dolly, I'm sorry," he said, then realized it wasn't enough. "You've got to understand that *Mamm* is always on the lookout for someone for me or Kolton. I've gotten so used to trying to sidestep her schemes that I guess I see them everywhere."

"Your mother is a lovely lady who wants to see her children happy. Is that a crime?"

"N-n-no."

"Maybe you should stop acting as if she's a criminal." She looked over her shoulder at him, and he saw tears in her eyes. "Me, too."

Shocked, he took her by the shoulders and sat her behind the counter. He flipped the switch on the electric teakettle, then pulled her favorite cup off a shelf and dropped a tea bag in it.

"I'm sorry, Dolly," he said as he filled the cup with boiling water. He set it in front of her.

"I'm not usually a blubber-puss." She stared into the darkening water.

"What's going on? You can't be this upset because I accused you of matchmaking."

"I'm not. It's…" Her voice faded.

He turned to see Emma on the interior stairs with Josie in her arms. Sorrow lengthened her face, and he wondered if she was seeking comforting words to offer Dolly.

As he was.

"It's Gil," Dolly continued. "I'm not sure what's going on with him. Not with his physical injuries. Those are straightforward, and the doctor says they'll heal fine. It's what he's been talking about lately." She raised her cup, then put it on the table untasted. "He was gung-ho to start the bakery, then he decided we should change business models. We were going to be sporting-goods store with a sideline for adventure tourism."

"I thought you were happy with that decision." Tyler glanced at Emma, who was listening without comment.

"I was. I *am*. I got to the point where I hated getting up at three a.m. to start bread and doughnuts." She paused as Emma came down the stairs and sat next to her. When Josie held out her arms, Dolly slid the little girl onto her lap and gave her a gentle hug. "I loved decorating cakes and dipping doughnuts, and I adored our customers. When I learned they liked the same treats I enjoyed baking, I thought I'd found the perfect life."

"Then Gil got the notion of a sport shop," Emma said.

"Yes." Dolly raised her eyes. "He said he'd never seen a man who enjoyed his life as much as you do, Tyler, and he wanted to enjoy his life, too."

Tyler pulled out a chair and sat. "Gil changed the shop because of me? That doesn't make sense."

"It does to Gil." Dolly sighed. "Or it did. All he can talk about now is a storefront available in Pagosa Springs."

"What?" Tyler asked at the same time Emma did, then she asked, "Where's that?"

"Out past Crestline," he replied. "You can't get

there from Crestline. You have to go northwest and then through the Wolf Creek Pass. Dolly, why's he interested in Pagosa Springs before you even open this store?"

"That's the question, isn't it?" Dolly handed Josie to Emma and stared into her cup. "He won't tell me because he says he wants it to be a big surprise. If you want to know the truth, I'm worried this will keep happening. He'll keep looking for the next exciting thing and leave the rest of us—leave me!—playing catch-up." Again, she looked at Tyler. "Has he told you what he's planning?"

"Nothing."

"Is that how he usually acts?" Emma asked.

Tyler shook his head at the same time Dolly did. "No, he blabs to everyone who'll stand still long enough about his big plans. He's proud of what he sees as his next step toward success."

"Maybe having him act differently means he's not going to do what he's done in the past." Emma gave them a faint smile. "Okay, that was confusing even to me. What I meant to say is that keeping what he's doing close to the vest—"

"Could suggest he's not about to turn this shop into an art gallery," Tyler said, finishing for her.

"An art gallery?" Dolly's eyes grew wide. "Has he said something about doing that? I love Gil, but he can't draw even an accurate conclusion."

Dolly's attempt at humor was a sign she was regaining her composure.

Tyler wished he could get his own back. "Don't worry," he said, though he knew words were useless. "You've got me to help as long as you need."

Dolly gave him a faint smile, but Emma flinched. Why?

He wasn't sure how to ask, so he took the dolly back to the barn. He paused to pat Emma's horse. The rain had slowed to a drizzle, matching his dreary mood.

"Hey, Tyler!"

At the shout, he saw two friends walking toward him. They paid no attention to the rain that had slicked their hair to their heads. He saw their jeans and sweatshirts that were emblazoned with Ski Everest and Olympus Mons Ski Team on the fronts. He doubted either Cal or Tex would ever tackle slopes in the Himalayas or on Mars, but the shirts fit their adventurous natures.

"Don't you know enough to get inside out of the rain?" he returned.

"You know," Cal said in his deep voice that resonated like thunder, "we're hoping it'll turn to snow."

"Getting too late in the season for that."

"Naw," Tex replied in the drawl that had given him his nickname. The short, stocky man was from California, while Cal had grown up in Vermont. "The old-timers say there's always a last snowstorm in the valley when you least expect it."

"Uh-huh." Tyler opened the passenger-side door on the truck and reached in to begin the complicated task of removing Josie's car seat.

"You're giving up?" Tex rested his hand on the truck's wet hood.

"Giving up what?" He straightened, the seat still half-hooked in place.

"Spring skiing."

"I didn't say that."

"You didn't join us last Monday, or the one before." Cal moved to stand behind his shorter friend.

"My boss got hurt, so I've been working extra hours as well as trying to help Kolton with his new bison."

"Excuses, excuses." Cal shook his head. "We're heading up to Breckenridge tomorrow. The spring skiing's supposed to be great there. You want to come?"

Tyler didn't hesitate. The burden of Emma's peculiar silence on the way home from Crestline hung over him like a storm cloud. He wanted to escape it, so he said, "Sounds like fun!"

Chapter Ten

Excitement buzzed around the open arena as the crowd gathered for the first rodeo of the season in Lost River. The space was large enough for everyone in town three times over, but there were only a few open seats as the clock counted down toward six thirty and the beginning of tonight's events. In the space between the tiers of bleachers, dirt had been raked smooth. Any puddles left in the wake of the melting snow had disappeared.

Around the outer edge of the ring were pens of various sizes. Emma wasn't sure which animals would go in each one. A third of the events would be competed that evening because the rodeo was scheduled to run over the weekend. After about two and a half hours of competition, the audience would be invited to pour onto the town's Main Street to visit the various businesses open to serve food and drink, as well as enjoy concerts and other performances. The partying would continue past midnight.

Emma watched the preparation in the ring

as animals and competitors got ready for their events. She tried to relax because the past two weeks had been filled with work, so much work, she'd barely had time to catch her breath or some sleep. Other customers had shown up at her door, asking her to make them special clothes for the rodeo weekend. She'd agreed to everyone's requests at first, but then had to turn away work. She simply didn't have time. Most people were willing to wait, as long as she could finish shirts or skirts or vests for them by the next rodeo in August. That event, with professional entrants, was the biggest rodeo in the valley all year, and she'd begun to believe that everyone within five square miles wanted her to make them something special to wear.

She'd been working in the shop as well. Most of the shelves and the new display cases were filled with merchandise now, but there were other tasks to finish. She heard Dolly and Tyler downstairs until past midnight most nights. Gil stopped in, doing what little he could while propped on crutches. He seldom lasted longer than an hour or two before he had to get off his feet. Yesterday, Dolly had been alone at the shop and had asked for Emma's help. The shopkeeper hadn't said where Tyler was. However, Emma knew he'd been working without a break for the past two weeks.

Just as she had.

She wondered if he'd used the day to sleep in and maybe take a nap and then head to bed early. That's what she'd do if she could steal a day off.

At the thought, she yawned. Beside her, Dolly and Gil were talking to a man and woman sitting to their left. They'd introduced her to the couple, who owned an auto-body shop in town. It was obvious the pair was more eager to see the demolition derby that was taking place the next afternoon than tonight's events, but she couldn't hear most of what they said with the multitude of conversations around her.

Stretching out her legs on the concrete riser in front of her, she admired the flags flapping in the breeze against the sky that was beginning to turn a richer blue as the sun headed toward the western peaks. A combined band of high schoolers and townspeople struck up toe-tappin' music, and she leaned forward, excited to see how her creations looked on several of the musicians. In the strong light from the sunset, the red-and-white piping she'd added to the shirts glowed like lasers and matched the jackets worn by the members of the high-school band.

"I'm sorry I'm late," a breathless voice said from her right. "*Danki* for saving me a seat."

In astonishment, she looked at Tyler, who was sliding into the seat next to hers. His face was red, and at first she thought it was because he'd run up the bleacher steps. Then she noticed paler circles around his eyes, and she guessed he'd been outside wearing goggles. Had he been skiing on his day off? If so, he looked well-rested.

The Yarwoods greeted him, and Gil tapped his crutch against Tyler's work boots. "Don't you know you're supposed to wear cowboy boots to a rodeo?" Gil asked.

What Tyler replied wasn't audible over the buzz in Emma's ears. She should say something, but words were stuck in her throat. Why hadn't either Dolly or Gil told her that Tyler would be joining them? She saw the twinkle in Gil's eyes as he gave his wife a gentle elbow, and Dolly wore a conspiratorial smile. Were they trying to make a match for her and Tyler?

She had to admit the idea had its appeal. He was handsome and kind, and Josie adored him. However, she couldn't forget—not for a second— that her life was an illusion. She wasn't the loving *mamm* of a beautiful little girl. Josie wasn't hers. Oh, how Emma longed to believe Sharon wouldn't *komm* to Lost River, but she'd witnessed how much her cousin cared about her daughter. Whatever had compelled Sharon to abandon Josie must have been horrendous.

Help her find her way to where she should be, Emma prayed as she had before. God would reunite *mamm* and *boppli* when the time was right. Only He knew the day and hour.

I hope it never arrives. The thought hastened

through her head before she could halt it. She asked God's forgiveness. How Sharon must grieve for the *kind* she had left behind! That Emma would be as sad when her cousin arrived for Josie couldn't change anything. A *boppli* should be with its *mamm*.

"Where's Josie?" Tyler asked.

Emma pasted on a smile. "Your sister is watching her."

"Mollie loves *kinder*, no matter their age. It's why she's a teacher."

"Did you ask her to offer to babysit tonight?"

He looked puzzled. "No, why would I?"

"Didn't you know Dolly invited me to attend with them?"

"I did, but I don't see the connection."

She took a deep, steadying breath. Accusing him of setting up this evening so they could spend it together would sound petty. He hadn't offered anything but friendship. Because it was enough for him?

It was a question she'd be smart not to answer. Instead, she asked him about the rodeo. He was answering when the horns in the band sounded a blast. Gates opened, and riders, clowns and flag-bearers burst out from every direction. All were teens. The parade went in multiple directions around the track. More than once, Emma thought there'd be a collision, but everyone knew where they should be and when, and it was as a true spectacle, as the American flag, the Colorado state flag and vivid banners fluttered in time with the band's raucous music. She stood to cheer as the parade's members rushed through the gates, leaving the area ready for the night's events to begin.

The bareback bronc riding was first. The contestants would compete to see who could stay on an unbroken horse for the full eight seconds. Emma was amazed there were other rules as well. After she watched the first contestant, who lasted less than three seconds on his horse, Tyler began to point out what the judges would look for in addition to the time requirement. She tried to watch for where the rider's feet were positioned during the rapid explosion of the bronc into the arena. She couldn't discern if the rowels, the spoked wheels on the spurs, were in front of the horse's shoulders, but she did manage to notice how the best riders kept their feet turned out during the short ride. She was astonished that the rider's free hand couldn't touch either the horse or himself while on the horse's back. Several riders slammed hard into the ground. She was relieved when each contestant waved to the cheering crowd at the end of his ride. What shocked her was learning the horses and riders were matched by drawing names or numbers before the event began.

"So they may never have seen the horse before?" she asked.

"Maybe not, or maybe they rode the same horse in an event last weekend. Not that any two rides are identical." Tyler chuckled. "Or so they tell me. Bronc riding is outside my comfort zone. I limit my risks to crossing a snow ridgeline while I try to avoid triggering an avalanche. We had to be cautious yesterday because the temps rose above freezing, and the snow slips when the underlayers get soft."

"You were skiing yesterday?"

"*Ja*. We went up to Breckenridge again."

"We?"

"Me and my skiing buddies. Most are *Englischers*."

"Oh." She wanted to ask how he could have left the store when there was much to do to make sure it opened on time next week.

Reminding herself that his life and his choices were none of her business, Emma settled in to watch the next competition. It was steer wrestling. She cheered and clapped along with the rest of the crowd in the bleachers as two riders and a pair of horses worked together. The hazer kept the steer going in a straight line, so the other cowboy, the bulldogger, could get close before jumping off the horse and forcing the steer to the ground with a combination of inertia and strength. She didn't dare blink, or she'd miss the whole thing. The teams worked in perfect unison, except for one where the nervous bulldogger set off too soon.

When the dozen teams of steer wrestlers were finished and a winner was announced to the cheers of his classmates from the local high school, Dolly said, "It's time for something to eat. Don't you agree?"

"Ja," Emma said at the same time as Tyler and Gil.

"Emma," Tyler asked, "would you lend me a hand—or two—to bring drinks and supper for us?"

"Lead the way." With a wave to her friends, she began to descend the concrete steps to the broad walkway that gave a clear view of the animal pens. She paused, leaning on the protective rail. A wiggling mass of calves was being herded into the pens below her. "Looks like the next event will be calf-roping." She trailed her fingers along the rail as she turned toward the stairs at the end of the next row.

"My favorite." Tyler stepped to one side to let a couple carrying enough food for ten people pass by.

"Why?"

"Because it's an event that's based on actual skills a cowboy needs. Cutting and roping are two essentials everyone on the range needs to know." He grinned. "Unless you've got bison. Those creatures are mountains who move when and if they wish."

She moved to the other side as more people

came from the opposite direction. "Kolton has challenges ahead."

"He's studied what he could before they arrived. Let's hope it's enough. I don't want to chase them along the road."

"Especially in the snow."

With a grimace, he started down the steps to the ground. "I don't like cross-country skiing, anyhow, and using skis to herd bison might be the silliest thing anyone has ever done."

"You could try skiing behind a buggy. I've heard about kids doing that."

"Kids like you?"

A terse laugh trumpeted out of her.

"What's funny?" he asked. "Were you always the *gut* girl?"

"I didn't have much choice. *Aenti* Pearl never let me go out with friends. Allowing me to ski behind a buggy? Never!"

He waited for her to reach the bottom of the steps before they walked together toward the food trucks, which were set in front of carnival rides being swarmed by kids. Striped awnings fluttered in the cool breeze, indicating that anyone who hadn't brought a coat would soon regret it.

"Your *aenti* was a termagant, ain't so?" he asked.

It was tempting to agree, but old habits couldn't be put aside. Instead, as they stepped over thick, electrical cords that powered the rides and trucks, she didn't give him an answer.

Tyler cleared his throat, then asked, "What are you interested in eating?"

"What's available?" She was glad he'd changed the subject.

"Anything you can imagine that's made with too much sugar or too much grease or, best of all, with too much sugar *and* too much grease."

Though she thought he was joking, Emma discovered Tyler hadn't been exaggerating. As they waited to order fried chicken, he asked, "Will you be attending services on Sunday?" Though his tone was casual, she could hear intensity behind the commonplace question.

"Why are you asking?"

"Because I'm curious."

"Are you going?" she returned.

"Why are you asking?"

Two could play that game. "Because I'm curious."

He cleared his throat again as if trying to decide what to say next, then a laugh burst from him. "I guess I deserved that, ain't so? *Ja.* I'll be at church on Sunday."

"Unless?" She edged forward a step when the people in line moved.

"I didn't say 'unless.'"

"I heard it. Are you hoping to go skiing? On a church Sunday?"

He looked at the heads in front of them. "My friends asked me to go, but I haven't given them an answer."

"What other answer can you give them than no?" She couldn't read his expression as she waited for his answer. When he didn't reply, she asked, "How long do you think you can straddle the fence between our world and the *Englisch* one, Tyler?"

"I'm not sure." Sorrow filled his words. "I do know I can't make the wrong decision for the wrong reasons. I've got to walk the path God created for me before I drew my first breath. Is it a plain life? Or among the *Englischers*? I don't know, Emma." He turned to her, his face grooved with regret. "You've got no idea how much I wish I did know."

"God can help you if you'll let Him. He's there for us when we need Him."

"I know that."

"But?"

"But nothing." He stepped away from her as the line moved. "I've learned it's useless to pray for something when I don't know what I want to pray for."

"Pray for guidance. That's what I do."

"What *gut* has it done you?" He spun on her. "Your life has been on hold for a year. Or has it been much longer while you were under your *aenti*'s thumb?"

She regarded him with disbelief. "Is that how you see my life? Like it's not moving forward in any direction?"

"Aren't you stuck while you wait for your cousin to return?"

"Tyler Lehman, you don't know what you're talking about! In the past year, I've made a life with Josie and I've started a business. I'm not stuck."

Sighing, he deflated. "I'm sorry, Emma. I shouldn't put my troubles on you. You've got enough of your own."

"It's okay," she said, though it wasn't. She wished he could find serenity within himself. Right now, she had that, but it wouldn't last if Josie was taken from her.

She made an effort, as he did, to act as if the harsh conversation hadn't happened. It was awkward for a few minutes, but soon they were carrying a cardboard tray piled high with burgers, chicken and sausages fried in peppers and onions, and topped with chili. Fries flopped out of their boat-shaped carriers with each step she took, and Tyler walked with care so not a drop of their chocolate milkshakes splashed out. Weaving in and out of the crowd, they returned to the Yarwoods.

Gil and Dolly praised their choices, and then they ate and cheered the calf ropers, who were younger than the contestants in the other events.

It was a large group, with only a few who failed to lasso their targets. Everyone applauded the attempts, anyhow, before a group of clowns began a hilarious dance in the middle of the arena.

Emma savored the sound of Tyler's voice as he teased her and the Yarwoods. Their laughter was the perfect match for the silly music the band played while the clowns cavorted and her heart did the same. She hoped the happiness would last a long time.

Much longer.

Tyler wasn't ready for the night to be over. He ignored how his legs ached from hours of skiing yesterday. On his last run down the mountain's side, those muscles had reminded him how many weeks had passed since he'd last skied. Getting caught up in working at the shop and helping Emma had kept him away from the slopes.

He glanced at the woman walking by his side, her head swiveling to take in the lights, sounds and aromas of the carnival that had been set up outside the arena. He didn't regret the time he'd spent with her and with Josie, though it had cut into his skiing time. He really didn't want this evening to end.

"How about taking a spin or two on the rides?" he asked as he paused, edging to the side of the stream of people so he didn't block its flow.

Emma stopped. "I don't know. Aren't they for *kinder*?"

"Some are, but the best ones are for kids and adults." A frisson of shock rushed through him. "Haven't you ever been on a carnival ride?"

She shook her head, lowering her eyes as she did each time a dark corner of her past was brought to light.

Putting his fingers under her chin, he lifted her gaze to meet his. "Because your *aenti* said no?"

"I never asked."

"Because you knew what her answer would be." He sighed as he grasped her shoulders. "It's over, Emma. What's happened has happened. You can't change it. The future is yours to decide, and you can make it whatever you wish it to be." Bending so his eyes were even with hers, he asked, "What do *you* want to do, Emma?"

Her lips parted, and he wanted to hear her say she wanted him to kiss her. To sample the warmth of her curved mouth as he held her in his arms. Would her heart beat in time with his? Could anything match its wild thump now, or would it leap out of his chest and twirl around in joy?

"I want to try one of the rides," she said. "I want to try one of the rides with you."

He waited for his sense of being blessed to fade, but it didn't. Her whispered wish reached inside him and urged him to recall his excitement about something like a carnival ride. He couldn't ignore the irony that a woman who hadn't had much of a childhood helped him remember his.

"That sounds *wunderbaar*." He held out his hand.

When she put her own in it, he walked by her side toward the rides covered with garish lights and surrounded by eager voices and music. He didn't release her fingers while they stood in line to buy tickets. As soon as he'd paid for them, he took her hand again as they passed the kiddie rides.

Tyler smiled when Emma waved to the young *kinder* riding in tiny cars and dragons around a short oval track. He was about to say that she would be able to bring Josie to the carnival next year, but he didn't. Too many times he'd seen Emma's eyes glisten with unshed tears when someone mentioned her and Josie doing something in the future. A dagger hung over Emma's head, ready to fall directly into her heart, every second of every day because her cousin could return and take Josie away.

Did anyone else realize how much strength Emma had to exert to get through each day when her whole life might crash down around her without warning?

He wasn't going to think about that tonight. Not when he could make sure she had a *gut* time.

"What's that?" she asked, pointing at an eight-armed ride that had cars at the end of each curved arm. The cars spun as the arms went up and down in a smooth pattern in time with the music coming from its center.

"It's called the Spider," he answered. "Do you want to try it?"

"*Ja*. It looks like fun, and it's not as high as the Ferris wheel."

"The Ferris wheel is fun."

"I've heard that people try to rock the seats at the top. No, *danki*!"

When it was their turn to board, Tyler assisted Emma in and then sat beside her as the safety bar was lowered. He was surprised to find the seats much smaller than he recalled, but he couldn't complain because that allowed him to sit close to her. He put his arm along the back to give her more space. The ride jerked as it moved to allow the next people to get on. His fingers dropped down over her shoulder, and he didn't move them away while she peppered him with questions about what the ride would be like.

"If I tell you, it won't be as much fun. Hold on!" He shouted the last when their car spun so their backs were parallel with the ground. He clamped one hand over hers on the safety bar.

She twisted to look in every direction. "This is amazing!"

"You won't think so if we're stuck here. Blood goes to your head."

"Did that happen to you?"

"When I was about ten. Kolton and I sat for a half hour while they got it running again. We were unsteady on our feet the rest of the day. I don't know how many times we said 'excuse me' because we'd collided with someone."

She laughed, then let out a little squeal as the ride began to move again, this time gaining speed.

Tyler watched her face during the ride. The breeze wafted soft strands of bright red hair across her face, which was alight with exhilaration. Each time the arm dipped, she shrieked and then laughed as it rose again. He doubted he'd ever heard such a beautiful combination of sounds. When the ride slowed, he was sorry.

"Can we ride it again?" she asked as their car turned toward the ground so they could get out.

"Whenever you want."

"How about now?"

"Now sounds perfect." He couldn't imagine words he meant more. Being with Emma and making her laugh *was* perfect. He intended to try to find a way to make their fun times together continue.

Chapter Eleven

Tyler yawned as he walked along Lost River's Main Street on a cool, sunny morning. Spring seemed unwilling to stay more than a few hours at a time in the valley. He should be glad because that meant the snow would remain longer in the mountains, and he could get more skiing in before having to pack away his equipment for the summer.

Today should be the last Monday he'd have to work. No, he'd agreed to work next Monday, when the store had its soft opening. The grand opening would be a week from Friday, but Dolly wanted to work any bugs out of the payment systems before the hoped-for crowds converged on the shop.

God, help Dolly's hard work pay off. The prayer was one he'd repeated every day since Gil's accident.

Would Gil be at the store today? His friend had mentioned at the rodeo that he was heading west to Pagosa Springs over the weekend, but the conversation had shifted before Tyler could ask him more. The chance to discuss it had been lost in watching the competition and then the fun Tyler had with Emma after.

He grinned as he strode along the street, greeting each person he passed. Emma had been smiling yesterday after the church service. He'd never seen her act comfortable with the *Leit*, and he wished he had figured out how to bring out her inner joy months ago.

As he passed the visitors center, Tyler looked at the barn quilt that hung on the barn behind it. His brother-in-law had painted the panels that made a gigantic square. Symbols of Lost River were arranged around the purple columbines in the center. Birds and plants and animals. A true introduction to the other quilts along the barn-quilt trail that was aimed at bringing tourists to the town and to various sites around the valley.

His steps slowed, and he continued to stare at the quilt. Noah, his brother-in-law, was an unconventional plain man. For half a decade, he'd traveled around the United States, creating barn quilts and the trails that brought tourist dollars. Somehow, Noah managed to have one foot on either side of the fence and felt comfortable among both plain folk and among the *Englischers* he worked with to create the works that hung along the quilt trails beginning to crisscross the San Luis Valley.

"Did I miss a spot?"

At the amused voice behind him, Tyler faced Noah. "You took a year off my life."

Noah chuckled, something he did more easily than when he'd first come to the valley. As Emma did, Tyler realized. Why hadn't he noticed the similarities between Noah's life and Emma's? Both had *komm* to Lost River as strangers and with *kinder*. Both had found a home.

Or, at least, he hoped Emma had.

"Sorry," Noah said, not sounding sincere. "I didn't have any idea you were wrapped up in viewing my work."

"Just thinking."

"A dangerous thing on a Monday morning." He tapped his temple. "Don't wear your brain out."

"No worry about that." He relaxed, glad Noah wasn't taking offense at every word as he had when he first arrived. "I set my mind in neutral Monday mornings. What brings you into town?"

"Mollie asked me to pick up construction paper for her scholars at the office supply store, and—" He grimaced. "I've got another meeting with the arts commissioners for this county and a couple of others. Everyone is jumping on the barn-quilt-trail train."

"That's *gut*, ain't so?"

"I'm trying to convince myself of that, but I'm not sure how many more I can do while in Lost River. Some sites are going to require me to travel, and I don't like leaving my family. Mollie has to stay until the school board finds another teacher."

Tyler took a deep breath, then said, "As long as she doesn't push the issue, the school board isn't going to do anything. She's such a *gut* teacher that they want to hold on to her as long as possible. They should have found someone months ago."

"I agree, but…" He raised his hands, palms up, with a shrug. Dabs of paint clung to his fingers. "Is the store ready to open?"

His brother-in-law wanted to talk about something else. Tyler went along. "Now that I've picked up the last display cases from Crestline, we're *gut* to go."

"Crestline? I was up there last month. I was speaking with the mayor—or the person whom they consider their mayor, though I doubt they've had anything as conventional as an election in years—and several other people about adding a few barn quilts to their other art installations. That's not going to happen until things get settled." He waved aside his words. "Sorry. I shouldn't complain that I've got opportunities. I know there's a happy medium out there. Mollie and I have to find how to balance it."

Tyler grasped the opening Noah had given him. "Noah, how have you balanced your life among the *Leit* and your life among the *Englischers*?"

"Not well, if you want to know the truth." He rubbed the thick beard along his jaw. "At first, I thought a lot about leaving the Amish. I might have except I believed I owed my *kinder* the chance to experience a plain life so they could decide which path to take."

"They weren't much more than *bopplin* when their *mamm* died. You were looking at years of waiting for them to be old enough to make such a decision."

"I know, but I convinced myself I had to give them the chance." He gazed across the street to where a group of revelers were laughing, as if the whole world was free of worries. "Now, I'm wondering if the voice of *gut* sense, as I called it, was knowing what God wanted for me as well as them. Are you moving into the *Englisch* world, Tyler?"

He had to be as honest as Noah was being. "I don't want to lose my connection with my family."

"Which is important. More important than I once understood." His smile was wry. "Some lessons I guess we have to learn the hard way."

"I've got the opportunity to keep people safe, as my brother does."

"As a volunteer firefighter, but you're not talking about that, ain't so?"

"No. For me, it would be working with the ski patrol."

When Noah didn't act surprised, Tyler guessed Mollie had already told him about the job Tyler had to turn down once.

His brother-in-law put a hand on Tyler's shoulder. "If you're asking me to point you in the right direction, I can't. God can, but nobody knows better than I do how hard it is to discern which path He's made for each of us. I wouldn't advise doing what I did."

"Which is?"

"Bumbling around until I almost lost everything *wunderbaar* that God had given me." He squeezed Tyler's shoulder. "God's gifts can slip through our fingers while we're trying to find our way instead of accepting His guidance."

Noah didn't say more before he walked toward the visitors center and went inside for his meeting, leaving Tyler to stand in the morning sunshine and consider his words.

Tyler did as he walked the rest of the way to Mountain Sports and Adventures, but he made sure he was smiling as he walked in. "Countdown started?"

Dolly looked up from the box she was opening. "I'd love to say yes, but my to-do list is about a million things long. If we can have our soft opening on time, I'm going to call the world-records people and let them know that the most impossible thing in the world has happened."

Instead of replying, he walked across the store to where she stood. Dark circles arced beneath her eyes, and her face was pale. Even her vibrant clothes didn't seem as bright as usual when every motion she made looked as if she were trying to wade through an invisible swamp. He didn't ask how early she'd started working. He suspected she'd been there all of last night.

He took her by the arm and steered her toward the back room. "Sit and have a cup of tea. I'll get rid of these last few boxes. Then we can start doing the touch-ups and decorating you want to do before we throw the doors open."

"Thanks, Tyler." She patted his arm. "I'll use the time to check the copy for our grand opening ad in *The Lost River Review*. Last time they sent it over, they had our phone number wrong." She shook her head. "My brain is going to implode with the details."

He resisted asking where Gil was. His friend had popped in on his crutches—and then left right away—on Saturday morning while Tyler and Dolly worked alongside Emma, and Tyler hadn't seen him since.

Tyler couldn't let this situation go on unchanged. Gil should have been in the store, working with his wife. The two were business partners, but Gil wasn't acting like that. Dolly was too exhausted to confront him.

It's not your business. You're an employee.

He knew that wasn't true. He and the Yarwoods were friends, and friends were honest with each other. As Noah had been forthright with him. He appreciated Noah's straightforward words, so he needed to be as open with Gil next time he saw him. He'd say—

A siren shattered the morning. Its sound reached a peak, threatening to pierce Tyler's ears. As it dropped and began to rise again, he heard a shriek from upstairs.

Josie!

He was running toward the interior stairs before another thought formed in his head. The siren's pitch fell a second time, but the cries from upstairs continued unabated.

Behind him, the phone rang, its sound drowned out by the fire siren, and he halted with his hand on the banister. Dolly burst from the back and snatched the phone at the same time she motioned for Tyler to hurry upstairs.

He didn't bother to knock. Instead, he shouted Emma's name as he threw the door open. She was holding Josie. Hearing distorted noise from the wall phone, he frowned. He'd thought it no longer worked.

"She's got an ear infection, so the sound hurts her." Emma bounced the *boppli* as she paced from one side of the room to the other. "It's okay, *liebling*. It's okay."

Josie screamed more loudly.

"Do you want me to try?" he asked.

"You might as well. She's not calming down for me." She started to hand him the little girl, but Josie grabbed Emma's dress and stuck like a bur. "It's okay, Josie. It's just a fire alarm." She shook her head. "I'm talking gibberish as far as she's concerned. She doesn't know what a fire siren is. All she knows is her ear hurts."

The sound cut off, and the silence stung his own ears for a second. The door slammed open.

Dolly burst in. Her eyes were wild. "A firefighter called. They're headed to your cabin, Emma! It's on fire!"

Tyler exchanged a glance with Emma, and he saw his confusion mirrored in her eyes. How could an empty cabin catch fire?

Two hours later, on Rimrock Road, Emma walked around what was left of the cabin she and Josie had called home for almost a year. Dolly had offered to watch the *boppli* and make sure she got medicine for her ear infection. Then Dolly had ordered Tyler to drive Emma out to the cabin. They'd chased after the fire trucks, which were visible in the distance on the straight, flat road leading out of town. There had been two fire trucks as well as an ambulance and a couple of police cars screeching down Rimrock Road. By the time the Yarwoods' truck had careened around a corner, where the flames could be seen shooting through the roof, the police had set up a cordon and were halting any curious spectators from getting close.

The driver of a battered car in front of the pickup had gotten out and started to protest. The cops had refused to listen, telling him to leave. The stocky, dark-haired man had snarled something Emma couldn't catch before getting into his car and peeling out in a cloud of dust and ash. The front end of the car had barely missed the truck.

Tyler had inched them forward. After rolling down the window, he'd asked, "Can we get through? She's been renting the cabin."

The cop, a burly man with silver hair, had frowned. "What sort of game is going on? The guy ahead of you said he's renting the place, but he couldn't produce any proof." He'd peered into the truck's cab. "Can you, lady?"

"I don't have the lease with me." Though Sharon had told her she'd put the paperwork in Emma's purse, Emma had never found anything but the keys for the cabin.

"You're going to have to leave," the officer had said. "We've got to keep this road open for first responders."

Tyler sat straighter. "My brother's with the fire

department. He can confirm Emma is renting this place."

The policeman had looked reluctant, but agreed to let Tyler pull the truck to one side. Tyler had gotten out and called his brother, who was jumping down from one of the trucks.

Scowling, Kolton had run over in his bulky turnout gear to reassure the cop that Emma and Tyler were being honest. He hadn't looked at either before he'd raced back to where his fellow firefighters were connecting hoses to the water truck. There were no hydrants this far from town, and they hadn't had time to search for an underground water tank.

Emma had had no choice but to watch from a distance as the high flames that had already claimed the roof were knocked down. Someone had given her a bright red-and-blue scarf to cover her mouth and nose.

Now, with the fire doused, everything and everyone reeked of smoke and wet wood. Somehow, the front wall had survived, though it was scorched. Water dripped down the logs and onto the front door that was ajar, as if waiting for someone to enter. Every window had shattered, and glass glittered on the ground like unmelted ice. It'd been spewed in a wide circle around the cabin.

The facade was a fallacy because behind the wall was destruction. The roof had collapsed, bringing down the loft with it. Any semblance to the well-worn house she'd known was gone. Emma doubted anything could be salvaged. Boards and the remnants of furniture were scattered around the yard. Had it all been pulled out by the firefighters, or had it been thrown out there before anyone arrived? A few lengths of wood were intact, but most had been splintered into pieces shorter than her fingers.

Tyler was closer to the road, staring down at something amid the destruction. He talked to some of the firefighters, a tense expression lengthening his face.

Emma bent to pick up a pot she recognized. It'd been in the kitchen, but she hadn't brought it with her to Lost River because it had been covered with rust where the enamel had been worn away. Now, it was blackened.

"Watch it. It may be hot," warned Kolton as he walked toward her.

He appeared imposing in his turnout gear, which was now stained gray and soaked. The heavy coat and pants looked like canvas, but she knew they must have been made of fire-resistant material. Carrying his helmet under his arm and shaking ashes out of his hair, he gave her a sympathetic smile.

"Danki," she said. "I should have thought of that." She looked past him toward the ruins. "The cabin blew up, ain't so? There's no other way ev-

erything could be scattered around like this otherwise."

Tyler's brother sighed. "That's what we suspect. Of course, we can't settle on a definite cause until after a full investigation has been done."

"How could it blow up? Tyler turned off the gas before Josie and I moved out. He double-checked that it was off. I saw him do it."

"Something else must have triggered the explosion," Tyler said as he came over to stand with them. His gaze swept the scene of the fire before he focused on his brother. An odd expression crossed his face, an expression Emma couldn't decipher. "But what?"

His brother shrugged. "Don't ask me, but the other guys are saying it was a gas explosion caused by propane building up under the cabin."

"Will you be the ones to determine the truth?" Tyler held his hands behind his back, but his shoulders were taut.

"No. There are inspectors who will sift through everything to get to the bottom of what happened. It'll take them a few days." Kolton frowned. "But I'd be amazed if it's anything other than an explosion. The debris all points to it. The only question is what exploded and why."

Emma's eyes were caught again by the blackened pan. Bending, she used a stone to tip the pan. Sunlight seeping through the smoke illuminated the interior to reveal a chunk charred to the metal.

"There's food in here," she said.

"How's that possible?" Tyler asked. "You told me that you'd cleaned everything so vermin wouldn't be lured inside, ain't so?"

"I did." Straightening, she looked along the road that led toward Lost River. "You heard that policeman. He said the guy in the car in front of us claimed to be living in the cabin. Could he have been?"

"Maybe," he replied, as if measuring each syllable. "Squatters will move into what appears to be an abandoned house. I didn't pay any attention to his car or his license plate. Did you, Emma?"

"All I noticed was that it was dirty and dented. I was focused on the fire." Her breath caught, but she swallowed the shock before it strangled her. How would Sharon find them now?

Kolton stared at the blackened cooking pan. "You'd better speak with the chief right away. He'll need to know this." He jerked his head to his right. "*Komm* with me."

As they crossed the yard, trying to stay out of the way of the firefighters finishing their work, Emma wished Tyler would take her hand as he had at the carnival. She yearned for the solace only he could offer her. She ached to reach out to grasp his hand, but halted herself when Kolton stopped and began speaking to another man.

That man wore a large helmet with a badge on the front that announced he was the fire chief. Smoke covered his skin, making his face the same color as his black hair. Behind gold-rimmed glasses, his dark eyes were in constant motion while he watched his firefighters making sure any stray fires had been put out completely.

"Chief, you need to hear what they've got to say," Kolton said.

Recognition eased the chief's stern face when he looked at Tyler.

Before he could ask who she was, Kolton added, "Chief, this is Emma Weaver. She lived here. Emma, this is Fire Chief Hino. Chikara Hino."

"Call me Chet," he said as he took her hands in his much broader ones. "I'm sorry for what's happened."

"I appreciate that," she replied, "but I'm living in Lost River now."

"I'm glad to hear that."

"You did an amazing job," Tyler replied, his eyes once more focused on the firefighters. "I had no idea how much work was involved in fighting fires."

The chief nodded. "If you want to know more, ask your brother. Or come and talk to me."

"I'll do that."

Before anyone else could add more, Kolton launched into an explanation about the pan

Emma had found and the possible ramifications. The chief's eyebrows dropped to the rims of his glasses as he scowled. With a sharp motion, he gave Kolton a silent order to follow. He halted Emma and Tyler with a terse thanks for their help.

"We'll take it from here," he said in a tone that suggested arguing wasn't an option.

Tyler put his hand on Emma's back and steered her toward Dolly's truck. She looked over her shoulder as Kolton and the fire chief went to examine the pan.

When they reached the truck, she reached for the door. He halted her by placing his hand on it. She looked at him, puzzled.

"Before we leave, I wanted you to see this." He brought his hand around from behind his back. In it was a small board that she recognized immediately. Not only from the drips of paint, but also the uneven lettering. *Sewing and Embroidery and Tailoring Done. Inquire Inside—Every Day Except Sundays.*

"That's the sign I put up when I moved in here."

"Ja." He handed it to her.

She examined it and realized the board hadn't escaped the ravages of the explosion. Three out of four corners were knocked off, and one of the holes she'd drilled near the top to hang it had been ripped away completely. Tears bubbled in her eyes, blurring the wood she held. It seemed a lifetime ago—someone else's lifetime—since she'd hurried to paint the sign, desperate for work so she didn't have to ask anyone for help to feed the *boppli* and herself. She had moved ahead from that frightened, emotionally battered woman. Not on her own.

Looking up at Tyler, who was regarding her with candid concern, she knew she'd still be stuck in the past, like an insect in a spider's web, if it hadn't been for him. He'd insinuated himself into her life, and he'd dared her to be a better version of herself. The version she saw reflected back at her from his eyes. Now, any day when she didn't spend time with him was as gloomy as a week of rain.

"I thought you might want it," he said quietly, drawing her attention back to the damaged sign.

"It's pretty beat-up." The trite words were easier to say than the thoughts speeding through her mind.

"There's some old lumber in the barn out behind the store. We can fix this or make you a new sign. Whichever you'd prefer."

Overwhelmed by his kindness all over again, she wanted to give in to the sobs knocking on her throat. It took every bit of her strength to push out the words. "Can we leave it here?"

"If you want. I don't blame you for not wanting a reminder of the fire."

"No." She raised her eyes once more and met

his as steadily as she could. "That's not it. Can we leave it and hang it somewhere?"

"What for?"

"I can tack a note on it so Sharon will know where Josie and I are." She held out the board to him. "Help me hang it somewhere, so she'll find it where she expects to find us."

"Why would you think that?" He didn't take the board from her, but instead opened the door. "You could be anywhere in the world, Emma. She didn't know you'd keep going to Lost River."

"She asked me to *komm* with her and Josie."

"*Ja*, but she didn't know you'd finish the trip after she left the two of you behind, ain't so? How could she be sure you wouldn't turn around and head home?"

"Because she knew I'd never go back! Not ever!" She clasped her hand over her mouth, knowing she'd said too much.

His eyebrows lowered again. "You've never explained to me why *you* left Indiana, Emma."

"No."

When she didn't add more, the silence stretched between them, sizzling like electricity along a high-tension wire.

Knowing honesty was the only choice, she said, "*Aenti* Pearl and I never saw eye-to-eye." She got into the truck, then set the board at her feet and pulled on her seat belt. If he didn't want to help her, she'd return as soon as possible and rehang the sign. She waited until he came around and slid behind the wheel, then added, "I know I should be grateful she took me in after my parents died. If she hadn't, I don't know what would have happened to me."

"Did she tell you daily—or more often—you should be grateful for her generosity?"

Surprise lifted her voice. "How did you know?"

"Your *aenti* Pearl isn't unique. Lots of people are glad to tell others what they should do and how they should feel about it."

She put her fingers on his arm. She knew she was being bold, but the pain in his voice overcame her own. Hers was so long-standing it had become habit. His was newer and fresh.

"I know," she said, "and it's hard not to heed what they have to say when I don't know if I'm right or wrong."

He put his hand over hers, and everything else in the world stopped as his gentle gaze enveloped her in a *wunderbaar* cocoon. The firefighters, the burned cabin, the questions of how and who—it all vanished as she submerged herself in his warmth.

"Emma," he whispered, "are you sure you want to rehang the sign?"

"Ja," she answered as softly.

"Even if it means losing Josie?"

"Ja." This time, her voice was no more than a breath that cracked with an escaped sob.

"Alright. If that's what you really want—"

"Of course, it's not what I really want. I want to have Josie in my life forever." She trembled as she spoke the words she'd never wanted to say. "But I've got to do what's right, Tyler. And that means helping reunite my cousin and her *kind*."

"All right," he said again. "I'll help you, though I'd rather do almost anything else."

"Danki."

When his fingers rose to cup her cheek, she leaned toward him, yelping when her seat belt cut across her.

The sweet moment was broken when he laughed, and she couldn't help but join in at the absurdity of their situation.

"I like to hear you laugh," he said as he started the truck.

"I like to hear you laugh, too."

"We need to do more of that." He stretched his arm across the seat as he began to reverse to where he could turn around on the crowded road.

"I agree with that."

He winked at her, but she saw powerful emotions still smoldering in his eyes. "Look at that! We agreed twice in a row. That must be a record." He edged the truck forward to avoid potholes and puddles. "Why not go for three and agree to go skiing with me and my friends the day after to-morrow?"

"Before the soft opening for the store?" she blurted, shocked.

"Dolly told me to take Wednesday off because she'll be doing, as she calls it, the pretty stuff, and I'll be in the way. My friends want to get in at least one more day of skiing. *Komm* with us?"

"I've never skied, Tyler."

"There are a few downhill places in Indiana. At least from what I've heard."

"I didn't go to them. Until I left with Sharon, I'd never been more than a dozen miles from home." Honesty propelled her to continue. "That was another reason why I jumped at the opportunity Sharon offered when she asked me to travel with her. I wanted to see the places I'd read about."

He lowered his voice as if he didn't want anyone to hear his excitement. "You need to visit the other side of the mountains, Emma. I don't know if I've ever seen any place as breathtaking as the peaks around Bison Springs. Some rise over fourteen thousand feet."

"You ski on such high slopes?"

"We have to be careful on the highest peaks to keep from causing an avalanche. It's one of the responsibilities we have when we're doing backcountry skiing on off-piste snow."

"What kind of snow?"

"Snow that hasn't been groomed so there are higher chances of snow sliding." He slowed the truck by the stop sign at the main road. Balancing his elbow on the wheel, he half turned to face her. "You've shown me what you love to do. Your embroidery. Let me show you what I love to do. Please."

Unable to resist his eagerness to share the snowy slopes he relished and her longing to spend time with him, she said, *"Ja."*

Chapter Twelve

A shout ran through the crowded van as Tyler traveled with a dozen eager skiers and one nervous novice toward Bison Springs Resort in the San Juan Mountains. He savored the anticipation among his *Englisch* friends. This might be their final day of skiing for the season. Many resorts were already closed, but the higher mountains had enough snow to make a few last, long, exciting runs.

Beside him on the hard seat, Emma was struggling to hide her anxiety. She wasn't doing a very *gut* job, because her eyes were huge behind her glasses. Her gaze kept darting from one side to the other as if she expected an avalanche to crash down on the highway. She didn't look plain. She wore vivid bright green ski gear. Dolly had insisted Emma have the best, though Emma had said used equipment would work for her.

Dolly had shaken her head and announced, "I'm not sending you out on such an important day with worn equipment."

Tyler chuckled under his breath as he recalled his advice to Emma. "Arguing with Dolly will get you nowhere. She's made up her mind. Say *ja* and smile."

She had tried, but had remained uncomfortable until Dolly told her to consider taking the clothing as a favor to the store.

Dolly had said, "Some of these items are ones we haven't had a chance to test ourselves. Our vendors have been eager for us to give them feedback on the samples they send to us. Try them, and let me know what you think. See? You'll be doing *me* a big favor."

Tyler hadn't believed Dolly's assertions, and he guessed Emma hadn't, either. He hadn't been sure if Emma would go. Only because Josie had been feeling better had she acquiesced and let his *mamm* watch the *boppli*.

His mouth tightened as he recalled the pleasure on *Mamm*'s face when he asked her to babysit. He sensed the questions she didn't ask. He didn't ease her curiosity because he wasn't certain how he'd answer if she spoke of his relationship with Emma.

How could he describe what he didn't comprehend himself? He knew he looked forward to being with her. She was woven into his thoughts and dreams. Spending time with her, or with her and Josie, was the best part of his days.

A roar of laughter resonated around him, and

he looked at his *Englisch* ski buddies. Two had already accepted offers to join one of the ski patrols to the north and were urging him to apply. He couldn't keep from imagining the amazing adventures waiting for them, protecting skiers and rescuing those who got themselves into trouble, playing cat-and-mouse with the mountains as they focused on avalanche mitigation. Nobody spoke of controlling avalanches, because those powerful forces couldn't be restrained.

Could he give up that life he'd longed for since he'd first read about the ski patrol when he was a kid? Even then, he'd known farming wasn't for him. His thirst for helping others and adventure in the snow had swept through him like an unstoppable virus. If there had been a cure, he didn't want it.

Now…he no longer was sure about anything.

Letting the voices wash over him, he gazed out the window at the mountains rising straight up from the curving road. *God*, he prayed, *I need You to show me the way You want me to take. I'm at a crossroads, and I don't know which way to turn.*

Stepping out of the gondola, Emma was relieved when she managed to get her skis out of the moving vehicle before they swept her off the platform. She stumbled forward a half step, then steadied herself in time to see Tyler emerge. His two friends who'd ridden up with them waved as the door closed and the gondola continued on its way higher along the mountain.

She'd been amazed when told they'd be taking the gondola lift up to the midlevel on the mountain. Tyler had talked of her using the lowest slope, but she realized the lowest slope *with snow* was five hundred feet up the mountain.

Cold air slashed her face, stealing her breath away. It'd felt like a cool spring day when they stepped into the hanging car at the base. Now, she stood in the middle of winter as gray clouds built up behind the peak and threatened to banish the thin sunlight.

"Don't worry," Tyler said as he motioned for her to follow him off the platform as another gondola swung to a stop. "It's not going to storm today."

"Is that what Kolton said?"

"No," he admitted with a guilty expression. "Just my hunch."

"I hope you're right."

He didn't reply as he led her along an asphalt path that had been kept clear of the snow banked on either side. Not snow, she saw, but ice.

She hoped it wouldn't be icy on the slope. As impossible as it was for her to imagine standing on skis in the snow, she doubted she'd be able to get to her feet on ice.

Two buildings, one large and one not much

bigger than a shed, were made of cedar. A few people were going in and out. Tyler explained the larger building was the lodge, a place that sold food and beverages and where people could relax after skiing. The other was equipment rental, which they didn't need because they'd brought their own.

Leading her around a line of people waiting to get onto a chair lift that ran at an upward angle to the left of the path from the gondola, Tyler didn't pause until they reached the bottom of a shallow slope. He sat on a long bench at the bottom and patted the spot beside him.

"Put on your skis, Emma." When she eased down next to him, he locked his on.

As he bent to check that she'd done hers correctly, she gazed up the mountain and at the nearby ones. The mountainsides were dotted with evergreens and underbrush waiting for the snow to melt; then it would burst forth with lush leaves and flowers. The mountains' tops poked up like rocky fingers, as if trying to tickle the sky. Tiny movements were, she realized with a gasp, skiers and snowboarders.

"The view is stunning," she said.

"Wait until you see it from higher up."

A single attempt to slide her skis through the snow behind Tyler warned her she had a lot to learn before she could do that. His seemed to be floating on the snow while hers were ready to tip her over.

Emma eyed the chairlift with wary eyes. "I'm not sure about that. Those chairs look as if you can slip right off them."

He jabbed his ski pole in the direction of the chair turning at the bottom of the lift. "There's a bar that drops down across your lap. It keeps you from tumbling out." With a chuckle, he pointed to where *kinder*, who couldn't have been more than five or six years old, were trying to maneuver their skis on a small hill that was more like a bump. "That's where we're headed. You won't use the lift until you learn the basics. To get to the top of the bunny hill, you've got to sidestep up by yourself. *Komm mol*, I'll show you."

He was patient and supportive while she tried to copy his motions. At the same time, he corrected her mistakes. Her head spun with his instructions and suggestions as he had her go the short distance over and over.

Each time, she struggled to get to the bottom without falling. Each time, she failed.

Emma brushed snow off her gloves. After rolling to her side, she pushed herself to her feet. How many times would it take before she could master what little kids were doing with alacrity?

"Okay, get yourself steady on your skis," Tyler said. "When you're ready—"

"I don't think I'll ever be ready." She waved

toward the steeper slopes. "I'm keeping you from your friends."

"They understand. Don't forget. We were all beginners at one time."

"I know." She gritted her teeth as she tried to move on the skis. She slid about five feet in the best snowplow she had managed so far and then lost control again, flopping into the snow. Some flew up, landing on her goggles. She took them off and squinted against the light bouncing off the snow, then knocked off the flakes before pulling the goggles back on over her glasses.

When Tyler moved toward her again, she tried not to be annoyed at his easy command of his skis. "You're letting one ski get ahead of the other." He bent over, wrapped his arms around her waist and lifted her up as if she weighed no more than one of his ski poles. "Let's try it one more time."

"I don't know if I have another time in me." She rubbed her backside. "Or on me."

"You do. You're not someone who quits when you face a barrier you've got to climb over." He smiled. "Or go through."

"You came to ski, not to spend the day picking me up out of the snow."

She'd thought he'd fire back a jest, but his voice was serious. "When I started skiing, my instructor was patient, because he knew no one in my family skied. I was coming to the mountain with only hopes. Later, I tried to thank him for the difference he'd made in my life. He told me to pay it forward and help someone else. He hoped I'd get as much enjoyment out of teaching as he did." His smile burst out. "He hoped teaching someone else would help me learn patience."

"You're going to need every bit of patience you've got if you want to help me stay up on these skis." She looked at them. "I appreciate how Dolly has outfitted me, but it's a waste. I'll never be able to repay her and Gil for their kindnesses to me and Josie."

"They don't expect you to."

"I know. Dolly told me I'd already earned everybody's kindness because I've pitched in while taking care of a *boppli* on my own." She stared at the snow. "What would she think if she knew I'd been false with her all along? I should have told Dolly and Gil the truth right from the first day."

He squatted beside her. "Why? What difference does it make now? In your heart, Josie is yours."

"Ja." Her voice broke as she added, "B-but what happens if…?"

"You've told me over and over to trust in God. Maybe you should heed your own words."

She rolled her eyes, though he couldn't see that behind glasses and goggles. "It's irritating to have my suggestions tossed back in my face. No, *you* are irritating to do that."

"Gut." He put his hands under her arms to steady her. "Okay, let's try again."

She couldn't answer as they stood face-to-face. Layers of clothing were between them, but she couldn't help but wonder if he could feel her wildly beating heart as she stared up into his face, which was half-covered by his amber goggles. His hands started to ease around her, but she shifted on her skis, sliding away. She waited for him to grasp her hands and pull her back.

He didn't. Instead, he advised her on how to stand. His voice was gruff. Was he upset at her? Did he think she'd edged away on purpose?

She risked a glance in his direction and wobbled on her skis. She looked down the hill again, but she'd caught his expression when he thought her concentration was elsewhere. He wasn't upset at her. He was upset with himself. She wished she knew why.

Tyler listened to the wind gaining speed across the mountain. Glad to be inside where it was warm, he carried two cups of hot chocolate across the lodge that was covered with cedar to match its exterior. The sloping roof was crisscrossed with beams. Cast-iron chandeliers dropped from it toward the circular fireplace in the center of the huge space.

After climbing down the steps of the hearth's round conversation pit, he handed one cup to

Emma, then sat beside her on the bright orange cushions. The conical vent rose to the roof high above their heads. The shape, he noticed for the first time, wasn't different from her *kapp*.

"The barista asked if you wanted whipped cream," he said as he set his cup on the built-in table beside him, "and I told her to go ahead and load it up. I hope that was okay."

She took a sip, then grinned past a foamy mustache. "It's perfect."

"You might want to drink it instead of wearing it." He handed her a napkin.

Wiping her mouth, she said, "Next thing, you'll be suggesting I wear a bib like Josie."

He chuckled, then sampled his cocoa. "That's the first time you've talked about Josie since we got here."

"She's been on my mind." She propped her stockinged feet on the hearth stones. "I've been so busy trying not to fall that I haven't said much more other than 'ouch.'"

"For the past hour, you've stayed up longer. Soon, you'll be trying one of the blue runs. Those are the ones for advanced beginners."

Looking at him, she said, "I don't know if I'll go skiing again."

"You don't like it?" He felt like he'd thrown his heart off the highest peak and was watching it careen down through the trees, getting battered on every bounce. Until now, he hadn't guessed how much he'd wanted her to share his love of the sport.

"I do like it." She smiled. "I don't know what the year will bring."

"Are you talking about Josie or work?"

"I'm not sure." She locked her fingers around her cup. "I used to know what each coming day would be like, because it'd be like the previous one."

"Maybe it's *gut* that you're not in that rut any longer."

"Maybe." She stared at the fire. "I'm glad I moved to Lost River and am becoming a part of the *Leit*."

That painful jerk on his heart happened again. It was simple for her to talk of belonging to the church community, and he found it easy to forget that when he was skiing.

"I'm thankful to God every day for what's been done for me," she continued when he didn't reply. "I could try out skiing today because I knew Josie would be in *gut* hands."

"*Mamm* said she'd be happy to watch her whenever you need her to."

"Your family has been kind to us." Her eyes shifted away, but not before he saw the tears filling them.

He hadn't meant to upset her. It had been *wunderbaar* to see her smile today. The more times she'd fallen, the harder she'd laughed. Today had been more fun than he'd had in a long time. That thought startled him because he'd never guess he'd be happier watching Emma fight to stay on her feet than to be going at full speed down a black diamond run with his friends.

"Emma…" He faltered.

She gave him a watery smile. "You haven't done anything wrong. It's just—" She hiccupped a sob, then quickly said, "I'm not used to having a family to depend on. I've been envious of those who do."

"You've had our community to support you."

"Support is one thing, and I'm grateful for it. Having a family, though, is something different. You speak often about Mollie and Kolton and your *mamm*, knowing they'll be there for you for as long as they're on Earth. Not just to help, but to share your common experiences from growing up under the same roof. I've longed for that for as long as I can remember, even before my parents died."

"You call them your parents. I haven't heard you call them *daed* and *mamm* more than once or twice."

"Of course, I have." She paused, taking a sip from her cup while she searched her memory. "Haven't I? *Aenti* Pearl didn't like me to talk about them. She got angry when I mentioned them. It became easier not to."

"What happened to them, Emma?" He took

her cup and set it next to his before he folded her hand between his.

Her hand quivered as she said softly, "It was a bizarre accident. I'd just turned seven when it happened, so I was at school. My *daed* had a woodworking shop next door to our house. My *mamm* was taking him his dinner when a tractor trailer tried to take the corner too fast and drove through the shop." She swallowed hard. "A neighbor came to school to alert our teacher, who stayed with me until my *aenti* arrived. She took me to her house immediately."

"So you never went back home?"

"No."

"How about for the funeral?"

"I wasn't allowed to attend that."

"Why not?"

She sighed and shook her head. "No one ever said. Later, I told myself my *aenti* missed them, too, and that speaking about that day was too painful for her."

"That was generous of you."

"I thought—at first—she was a generous person. I learned soon she saw me as a means to an end. At first, she was pleased to have everybody tell her how special she was to take in an orphan. That was before she became obsessed with me making money to pay for my upkeep."

"To pay for more than that, I suspect, after seeing your skilled sewing."

"Ja." She smiled weakly. "Don't make me out to be an Amish Cinderella."

"I'm not a Prince Charming, either."

"I've seen you charm plenty of people. That gal in the food truck at the rodeo thought you were pretty charming."

"Do you mean the one who was older than my *mamm*?"

Her laugh eased his discomfort. "Don't you think Prince Charming charmed *all* the ladies?"

"Can't say I'm an expert on the subject." He looked at their feet propped next to each other on the stones. "Especially because I can't charm my brother."

"Kolton wants you to work more on the farm?"

"Ja." He shuddered at the thought.

Seeing the dismay digging lines into Tyler's brow, Emma could discern what he hadn't said. Tyler didn't want anything to do with farming. His life was in the mountains and working at the shop. Guilt had clamped around him.

Oh, how well she understood that. She'd learned to enjoy sewing, but her *aenti*'s demands turned it into drudgery. Only when Emma had needed a way to provide for herself and Josie had she returned to sewing, doing work by hand until she'd made enough to buy her secondhand machine.

"Will you work on the farm?" she asked.

"I should. It's expected of the eldest to be the one to step up and take over the family and the family business."

Now, it was her turn to have her brow wrinkle with powerful emotion. "Why do you say that? In most plain families, the youngest takes over the farm once the parents retire to the *dawdihaus*. The youngest is old enough, so it's the perfect time for the transition from one generation to the next."

"That's when a *daed* doesn't die before his time."

"Your brother isn't a *kind*. He's a grown man, and he loves farming. You can see it when he talks about raising bison and making improvements to the land. There's a glow in him." She smiled. "As there is in you when you talk about being out on the slopes. God puts a light in each of us, creating a fire in our hearts. When we're where we're supposed to be and doing what we love, His light shines through to let us share our joy and His joy."

"Like when you talk about Josie."

She nodded, her eyes stinging with tears. "*Ja*. Taking care of Josie is what makes me happy."

"You and Josie are a family."

His words startled her. Though she'd longed to believe the two of them were meant to be together, she'd seldom dared to connect the word *family* with the life she was living now. She'd longed for a family for years, but hadn't recognized when one was dumped literally into her lap.

A family.

Emma Weaver and her family. Her *daughter*.

She pushed the thought out of her head. Josie wasn't her daughter. She was Sharon's.

Leaning toward her, he dropped his voice to a gentle whisper. "What did I say that upset you?"

"About me and Josie being a family."

"You are, ain't so?"

"I'd like to think we are, but I know how everything can fall apart in a split second. If Sharon looks for us in Lost River—"

"Don't you think if she wanted Josie, she would have shown up by now?"

"I don't know, Tyler. I honestly don't know." She closed her eyes because she couldn't bear to see her sorrow reflected in his face. "Maybe if I'd had a chance to know Sharon better, I could guess. I spent less than a week with her."

"I didn't realize that."

His surprise brought her eyes open again, and she gave him a self-deprecating smile. "Because I didn't tell you. That I left the only home I had to go across the country with a woman who was pretty much a stranger isn't something I'm proud to admit."

"It was a *gut* decision, ain't so?" He offered her the unfinished cup of hot chocolate before picking up his own and taking a sip. "You've got the family you never had."

"I do remember when family meant something and someone special. More than one someone."

"You've tried to forget that?"

"Ja," She tightened her hold on her cup, then loosened it before she crushed the thin cardboard. "It was the best way I could survive living with my *aenti* Pearl. I had to forget what a family could be."

"Did you?"

She shook her head. "How could I? Everywhere I went I saw people who had what I wanted, a family who loved and cared about each other. Not a family filled with regrets."

"Yours?"

"Ja, and *Aenti* Pearl's. She must have regretted agreeing for her and my *onkel* to be my guardians."

"She was married?" He shifted to face her, and again the rest of the world fled.

She looked into her cup ringed by layers of chocolate. "My *onkel* died a few years after my parents. He was a *gut* man who didn't dare to express his opinions. He was as kind to me as he could be without irritating her."

"Was he scared of her?"

An uneven smile vacillated on her lips. *"Ja...* No—no, I don't think so. *Onkel* Conrad was a *gut* man, but he never said anything against my *aenti*. He'd gotten accustomed to her complaining. Anything she said went in one ear and out the other without him registering it." She sighed. "On the rare occasions he did notice me, he acted surprised I was there. He was kind to me in the way he was kind to the old cat that had moved in and refused to leave."

"You stayed, too."

"I didn't have anywhere else to go."

He shook his head. "You're resourceful, Emma. You could have figured something out."

"I'll never know because I stayed."

"And survived." He drained his cup and set it on the table. "Your cousin saw that and realized she could leave her *kind* with you, knowing you'd love Josie as you'd wanted your *aenti* to love you."

"Sharon had to see how much I doted on Josie. I kept asking to feed her, to hold her, to rock her, to change her."

"Like I do when I visit?"

"*Ja*. It's a *gut* thing you do because Josie is excited to see you. You're *wunderbaar* with little ones, Tyler."

"As you are." He shook his head. "I don't get it. You're thrilled to have Josie. You love her, but you keep talking about giving her to someone who abandoned her."

"I'm not her *mamm*."

"You're the only one she knows!"

"Stop this!" She got to her feet, picked up both cups and carried them to the trash. After tossing them in, she went into the ladies' room, where he couldn't follow her.

Emma stayed there until it was time to leave. She rushed to get on the van so she wouldn't have to sit next to Tyler. When she chose a seat next to one of his friends, the *Englischer* started to get up. She told him it was fine and leaned her head against the window. Closing her eyes, she pretended to fall asleep. She kept up the pretense on what seemed like an endless trip back to Lost River through heavy rain, opening her eyes only when the driver announced the next stop was the house where Tyler's *mamm* lived with her second husband.

She expressed her gratitude to the *Englischers*, including the van driver. Hurrying out of the van, she quickly collected her ski equipment from where it was leaning next to Tyler's on the side of the vehicle. She carried it through the rain, which was turning to sleet. After putting it in her wagon and pulling a tarp over the skis, she hitched up Apricot while Tyler was ensnared in conversation with his friends.

If they kept talking, she could get Josie and leave before she had to face him again. Frustration and anger billowed within her like a huge thunderhead.

She was on the walk up to the door when Tyler

called her name. She stepped onto the porch to get out of the rain and waited for him to do the same.

As if their conversation hadn't had a break, he said, "You've got to face the facts, Emma. You can't pretend they don't exist."

"Which facts are those?" She kept her head high so tears didn't rise into her eyes.

"The longer Sharon is gone, the less likely it is she'll ever show up. You've got to face the facts. Not as you want them to be, but as they are!"

Shocked by the coldness of his voice, she gasped. His face was rigid. Where was the gentle-hearted man who made Josie giggle each time he made a silly expression? Now, he looked like an Old Testament patriarch, ready to call down God's vengeance on miscreants.

She girded herself for being harangued and told she was stupid and useless and a burden on everyone who knew her. Her *aenti*'s voice exploded out of her memories, ripping apart the guards she thought were in place. It was as if time had collapsed, and she was a *kind* once more, terrified of the woman who controlled her life.

No! Emma wasn't that frightened, grief-stricken little girl any longer. She had escaped the torture of being told she was less than useless. She wasn't going to let anyone, most especially not Tyler, whom she'd dared to believe was as different from *Aenti* Pearl as was possible, treat her like that.

"*Danki* for sharing your opinion." Emma saw she'd shocked him into silence with her cool answer. Without another word, because she feared her voice would crack with unshed tears, she rushed into the house, collected Josie, thanked Viola for watching the *boppli* and was out the door before she had to say anything more. She got into the wagon. Slapping the reins on Apricot, she turned it out of the yard and north toward town.

The rain was getting thicker and thicker, more ice than water. Emma glanced back a couple of times and didn't see anyone in pursuit of her. Tears fell as hard as the rain, but were burning hot.

Slowed down by the storm, the wagon didn't reach Lost River for two hours. Emma's tears were used up before she reached the shop. It wasn't easy to maneuver the wagon around the car parked behind the Yarwoods' pickup. Both were shapeless lumps covered with snow. In the barn, she unhitched Apricot, dried her off and fed her.

She left her equipment in the barn. Tomorrow, she'd return it to Dolly and hope her friend could sell it so Emma didn't have to see it again.

Gathering up Josie, she unzipped her coat and put the little one inside without waking her. It was the best protection she could offer when the

sleet was clustering into snow. That it was snowing seemed impossible, but no more impossible
than Tyler's callous words. Words she wouldn't
have believed he could speak, except she'd heard
them herself.

Emma went up the stairs with caution. She
didn't want to slip when she was cradling the
sleeping *boppli* in her arms. Reaching for her
door, she frowned with the knob turned. Hadn't
she locked the door before she'd left to take Josie
to the Zehrs'?

It was too cold to stand on the narrow landing
and ponder. Using her toe, she pushed the door
open and stepped inside. Every light in the main
room was on, electric as well as the battery-operated lamp by the sofa. What was going on?

As if she'd asked that question aloud, she heard
her name called. She looked toward her sewing
room. A silhouette—a female silhouette—filled
the doorway. The figure stepped into the light,
and Emma gasped.

"Sharon!"

Chapter Thirteen

"What are you doing here, Sharon?" Other questions burst like spicy jalapeños on Emma's tongue, but she didn't let them past her lips. She didn't want to send Sharon fleeing again.

Fleeing?

Once the word formed in Emma's mind, it refused to be ignored. For the past year, she'd convinced herself that her cousin had made her decision to abandon her *boppli* after careful thought. She'd been wrong, she realized, as she saw Sharon's trepidation now. It matched how her cousin had acted on the bus in the last minutes before she vanished. She was looking around and not meeting Emma's eyes.

Then her shock ebbed as dread rolled over her like a tsunami. Sharon was there to get Josie.

In her mind, she heard Tyler's arguments that the longer Sharon was gone, the less likely her cousin would *komm* back. When she could look her cousin in the face, she realized why his words had angered her. Not because she believed they were untrue, but because she prayed they were. She hadn't wanted to admit how much she wanted the *boppli* in her life, to love her for the rest of her days. Sweet little Josie, who couldn't remember her true *mamm*.

Agony struck her, and she swallowed hard. Holding Josie close, she realized she had her ski coat on. She set the sleeping *boppli* on the sofa, shrugged off her coat and hung it up while she waited for her cousin to answer. After pulling off her boots, she put them on the plastic tray by the door.

"I've come to see you," Sharon said as Emma padded toward her.

"Along with Josie, of course." She turned toward the couch, where the little girl was blinking as if waking from a dream. From a dream into a nightmare? She thought of the day her teacher had handed her over to *Aenti* Pearl. No explanation except her parents were gone and she had a new home. When she'd asked for *Daed* and *Mamm*, she'd been told they were with God and it was His will for them to be called home. She hadn't understood any of it then, believing her beloved parents had deserted her, leaving her with a heartless woman who didn't hide how little she wanted Emma.

None of that was going to happen to Josie. The *boppli* was too young to comprehend what was happening. Also, Emma intended to remain a

part of Josie's life. Somehow. If Sharon planned
to return east, she'd have to go as well, leaving
behind everything and everyone in Lost River.
The anguish hammered her stomach again. *God,
please don't make me choose between Josie and
my life here.*

"Of course. Josie." Sharon's answer was un-
emotional, shocking Emma anew.

"*Komm* and see her." Emma managed a smile.
Did it look as grotesque as it felt? "She's missed
her—"

"I'd love to see your little one, cousin." Her
intense gaze warned Emma not to correct her.

What was going on? Why had Sharon returned
today when Emma's world was already falling
apart? Why was she acting as if Josie was Emma's *kind*? If it was meant to be a joke, it was a
horrible one.

After picking up the *boppli*, Emma removed
Josie's outer clothing. She tossed the garments
onto the sofa and turned to face her cousin. Seeing the candid hunger in Sharon's eyes, she asked,
"Would you like to hold her?"

Sharon's arms rose, as if she was hypnotized,
and she reached for the little girl.

Josie let out a shriek and hid her face against
Emma's neck.

"Give her a moment," Emma said. "She's had
an ear infection, so she's not herself. She's not
usually scared of…"

"Strangers," Sharon said. When Emma started to protest, she said, "Save it for later, okay?" Again, her gaze slid away, and her voice dropped to a whisper. "I need to talk to you before you say anything else about her."

"Sure. I thought—" She gasped when a man stepped out of the shadows in her unlit kitchen. "Who are you?"

Sharon rushed to the dark-haired man's side. He wasn't much taller than her cousin, but appeared to be built of solid muscle. The sleeves of his windbreaker were loose, but it was so tight around his bulky torso Emma wouldn't have been surprised to hear him complain his circulation was cut off. The zipper strained as he moved to drape his arm over Sharon's shoulders. Sharon smiled, but his face, with its narrow mat of black beard, remained expressionless. But then his brown eyes swept over Emma. She saw surprise, then an emotion she couldn't read in them. He seemed familiar. Had she seen him in Lost River? Without Sharon? Her cousin hadn't tried to see Emma and Josie until now. Something didn't add up.

"Who's she?" he demanded instead of answering Emma's question.

Before Emma could reply, Sharon said, "That's my cousin Emma. I told you this was her place, Ron."

He took a large bite of the sandwich he held

in his massive hand. Emma had been so shocked by him being in her home she hadn't noticed he was carrying what looked like the contents of half a jar of peanut butter between the two slices of bread. That bread had been for her supper tonight.

"You said she was Ay-mish."

Emma winced at the mispronunciation, but her cousin didn't react.

"She is." Sharon wore an unsteady smile.

"I didn't know Ay-mish went skiing."

"She—"

Knowing she was being rude, but unable to halt herself when her time with Josie might be running out, Emma said, "We *Amish* do all kinds of things. Such as wondering who you are and how you got into my apartment when the door was locked."

"It wasn't locked," the man snarled. "You can't accuse us of breaking and entering."

"I'm not." She chose her words with care. The man seemed to have a hair-trigger temper, and she didn't want to do anything to set him off. "I guess I must have forgotten to lock it on my way out." She knew she had secured the door, but she wasn't going to insist her cousin be honest about how she'd gotten inside. Later, she'd ask. For now, she needed to know why Sharon was there with a stranger. Looking at her cousin, she gave her what she hoped was a goading expression to introduce her to the man by her side.

Sharon took the hint. "This is my fiancé. Ron Timmerman."

"Fiancé?" Her cousin was planning to marry an *Englischer*? For the first time, she noticed that Sharon wasn't dressed plain. Instead, she wore jeans and a gray sweatshirt with *Black Hills* on it in red satin letters. "I guess I should say congratulations."

"It's okay," Sharon said. "I understand you're not used to people announcing their engagements outside of a church service." Again, she gave Emma a pleading look.

Emma nodded, trying to forestall her own questions. Why was Sharon acting as if Josie belonged to Emma? Hadn't she told the man she planned to marry that she'd been raised plain?

"Ron, I'm glad you've made yourself at home." She patted her ski pants. "I need to get changed."

"You sure don't look like any Ay-mish I've ever seen," he said before chomping more of his sandwich. At the rate he was going, it'd be gone in four bites.

Sharon frowned. "Ron, we talked about this before. It's pronounced *Ah-mish*, not *Ay-mish*."

With a shrug, he said, "I don't know why you care. She's the one who's Ay-mish, not you." He paused as he raised the sandwich to his mouth again. "How come she's Ay-mish, and you aren't?

I thought you were cousins." His eyes brightened. "Is it like me being a Cincinnati Bengals fan and my cousin liking the Cleveland Browns?"

"Something like that." Sharon grasped Emma's shoulders and turned her toward the bedroom, not giving her a chance to react to her fiancé's absurd comment comparing football teams to a way of life. "C'mon. You promised me you'd show me that new dress you made. I can't wait."

Emma was about to protest she didn't have a new dress, and she couldn't have told Sharon about it because she hadn't heard from her cousin since Sharon had walked away from her and Josie. Sharon steered her into the bedroom and shut the door.

Putting her finger to her lips, Sharon glanced toward the closed door. "We need to talk." Her voice dropped to a whisper. "Quietly. Quickly."

"Start by explaining where you've been." She put the *boppli* on the bed, then sat and began to slide off her ski pants.

"No time for that now." Sharon grabbed a light blue dress off its peg and tossed it to Emma. "You've got to listen to me."

"That's what I want to do. I want to listen to why you deserted your own—"

Sharon raised her voice enough so it would be heard on the other side of the door. "This is so cute, Emma. You really know how to sew pretty things." Her face tightened as she whispered, "You can't let Ron know Josie is mine."

"What?"

Waving to her to keep her voice down, Sharon then motioned for Emma to finish changing. Emma complied, pulling on fresh socks and her sneakers, but demanded that her cousin explain why she was planning to marry a man who didn't know about her *boppli*.

"It's complicated," Sharon replied.

After closing the snaps on the front of her dress, Emma reached for her black apron and pinned it in place at her waist. "How complicated can it be?"

"You heard him, Emma." Sharon began to pace at the foot of the bed. She kept glancing at Josie, but didn't move toward her. "He doesn't know I was plain."

"Why not?"

"I haven't told him. It doesn't matter because I'm not plain any longer." Her mouth tightened into a bleached line. "They don't want me, and I don't want them."

"They? Who is they?"

"Someone started a rumor that spread through community after community as if it'd been published in *The Budget*."

"What did people say?"

"That I don't know who Josie's father is."

Emma flinched when Sharon didn't use the

Deitsch word for "father" as most plain folk did when they spoke English. Then she realized that they could have been having this conversation in their native language and Ron wouldn't be any the wiser.

When she said that to her cousin, Sharon said, "I can't take the chance he'll overhear me. You've got to understand, Emma. He treats me nicely. Not like Josie's father." Her mouth tightened to a straight line.

"Is that why you were running away?" Emma asked when her cousin remained silent. "Were you hoping to put an end to the relationship?"

"I was, but it didn't matter. I learned that when I got a call in Topeka."

"You had a cell phone?"

She patted her back pocket. "Of course, I had a phone. I'm not like you, Emma. You toe the line. You never questioned if you'd be baptized when you were old enough."

"I might have." She turned to brush her hair into its proper bun, not wanting her cousin to see her face. "I never had a choice."

"Your dreary old *aenti* made sure you stayed chained to a sewing machine." Sharon flung a hand out toward the wall. "Now, you've got another one. I thought you wanted to put that life behind you, too."

"I love sewing. It brings me great joy, a true gift from God."

Tyler's voice echoed in her head. *You've shown me what you love to do. Your embroidery. Let me show you what I love to do. Please.* She'd agreed to go and, to her surprise, had discovered skiing was fun. Then everything had fallen apart.

Emma picked up the *boppli*, who'd begun to whimper. When had Josie had a dose of medicine to fight her ear infection? It would be time for the next soon. "Tell me about the phone call you got, Sharon."

"It was from a friend." Sharon raised her hand to ward off Emma's next question. "Don't ask me who. I won't tell you because I don't want her to get into trouble. She told me Josie's father had died."

"You left us behind so you could return to Ohio for his funeral?"

"I couldn't go to his funeral because his family would have been there, and we didn't get along. But I needed to know if what my friend had said was true." She dropped to sit on the bed. "It was true, so I knew what I should do."

"You *should* have traveled to Lost River right away."

"There were things I needed to do."

"And you met Ron."

The first hint of a smile eased Sharon's strained face. "He's a good man, Emma. He's going to make the best life for us." She reached under her sweatshirt and pulled out an envelope. "This is for you."

Emma took it. "What's in it? Not the lease for the cabin, I hope. It's burned down."

"I know."

"*You* were living there."

"Why not? I paid for it, and you weren't there." Again, she looked away. "I saw your note and knew you'd moved here. I wanted to come and see you right away, but Ron..." A faint smile flitted across her lips. "He was hungry, so he insisted we go inside."

"And you turned on the gas?"

"Sure. We didn't want to freeze out there in that dump. It sure looked better in the pictures online."

Emma glanced toward the closed door. "So that was Ron out at the fire in the silver car, ain't so? Were you there at the fire, too?"

"Yeah, but the cop had a hissy fit, and we had to leave."

"Why didn't you *komm* here then?"

Sharon gave a shrug, her shoulders moving so slowly that Emma guessed they were as stretched as tight as her own. "Ron was furious about the cop, so he refused to stop here. We ended up driving all the way to Fort Garland, near the Sangre de Christos. This morning, we headed back here. I knew you'd open your door for us, so we came in and waited for you."

"By breaking in to my home?"

"Ron knows how to pick locks. It was cold, and I figured you wouldn't mind." She shrugged as if it didn't matter.

And it didn't, Emma realized, as she tried to soothe Josie, who was getting louder with her wordless complaints. "Let me get Josie her medicine. She's got an ear infection."

Instead of sympathy for her *kind*, Sharon said, "Listen to me before you go out there. In that envelope is the paperwork to give up my custody of Josie. I've signed all of it. She'll do much better with you than with me."

"You're her *mamm*."

"I gave birth to her, but you're her mother." A single tear rolled down her cheek. "She doesn't know me. If you won't do this for me, or for yourself, Emma, do it for her."

Looking from her distraught cousin to the *boppli* she held next to her heart, she realized she was getting what she'd asked for when she wished Josie would remain a part of her life. Sharon didn't want her daughter. She wanted Emma to raise her. It was what Emma had prayed for, over and over, but never had she imagined God's answer would come mixed with such sorrow.

As he stood in *Mamm*'s living room and listened to her talk with Kolton and her new husband in the kitchen, Tyler wondered if he could have guessed today would end up as it had. Had he been foolish to tell Emma about his doubts of living a plain life? He'd never breathed a hint of that indecision to his family or any of his friends, plain or *Englisch*. Many must have guessed because he was long past the age when most people decided to be baptized. *Mamm* had recently stopped dropping hints it was time for him to make that commitment. Had she given up on him, and was trying to be satisfied that two out of her three *kinder* had been baptized?

Today, he'd spilled his guts to Emma. She'd listened as she always did, not being judgmental, but asking insightful questions. Then everything had gone sideways when he'd prodded her to be as honest about her future. Had he been trying to help her face the truth about her irresponsible cousin, or had he instead been probing to discover if there was room in her life for him as more than a friend? He didn't know. Maybe it'd been both.

"Hiding won't get you the last piece of *Mamm*'s coconut pie," his brother said from behind him.

"The one you've already eaten?" He was proud when a hint of his usual teasing tone slipped into the words.

"*Ja*, that one." Kolton walked over to the window and peered out. "It's coming down hard. I'd better head back to the farm. I need to make sure the cattle are in the barn before it gets too deep."

"What gets too deep?"

"It's snowing. I thought that's what you were doing. Watching it."

Explaining how he was stuck in an endless loop of self-incriminations wasn't something he wanted to do. At last, as Kolton was pulling on his barn coat and reaching for the door, Tyler asked, "Any idea how much we're going to get?"

"A bunch. Maybe a foot. Maybe more."

"This late in the spring?"

Kolton's mouth twisted. "You know how it is. The later the last snow, the worse it'll be."

"So you've said."

"So your *daed* used to say." It was *Mamm*'s voice as she walked into the living room. In her hand, she carried a small bottle. "I pray you're wrong, Kolton."

"I'd like to be." He glanced out the window in the door. "I don't think I am."

"Then, Tyler, you'd better leave straightaway." She held out the bottle. "This is Josie's medicine. Emma left before I could give it to her. The *boppli* is going to need it."

Tyler took the small bottle, which was cool to the touch. "I'll get it to Emma."

"Tyler…" his brother began.

Looking at Kolton, he saw the dismay in his brother's eyes. Dismay and trepidation. Was Kolton being honest with them, or did he believe the storm was going to drop more snow than he'd suggested?

"I'll get it to Emma," he repeated. "If I leave now and take the buggy, I should be able to get there before it's bad."

Kolton grabbed his sleeve. "Be careful. It's already bad."

After heaving on his coat and putting the small bottle in a zippered pocket, he reached for his hat and gloves, glad he had his ski clothes with him. He pulled on his boots before he opened the door.

Wind and snow pressed in like a thousand tiny spears, cutting into his bare face. He nodded his thanks when *Mamm* pressed a thick scarf into his hands. Without another word, he took a deep breath, as if he was about to jump into the ocean. He stepped out into the storm that swallowed him and battered him—it was like being caught in a rising tide.

A frisson of fear sliced down his spine as he fought his way to the buggy. He prayed Kolton was wrong and this was no more than a vicious squall, but dreaded his brother would be right about the weather. Tyler wondered for the first time if he'd be able to get through the intensifying storm to deliver the medicine to Lost River.

Chapter Fourteen

Josie's screams rang through the apartment. Cuddling her, Emma tried to comfort the *boppli*, who kept tugging on her earlobe. She bounced the little girl in her arms as she walked from one side of the apartment to the other. Beyond the windows, the world was obscured by thick snow.

She should have made sure she had Josie's medicine before she left Viola's house. Being distressed with Tyler was no excuse not to think first of the *kind*. Knowing berating herself was useless, she couldn't halt herself from doing that in time with Josie's shrieks.

"How long is that going to keep going?" asked Ron after he'd finished off the last of the bread and peanut butter in another immense sandwich.

"She's not feeling *gut*." Emma was annoyed with his selfishness and disinterest in anyone but himself, but she found her cousin more vexing. How could Sharon sit and scroll through her phone when her daughter was in pain?

Then her cousin raised her eyes and met Emma's gaze for a half second. It was time enough to see that each of Josie's cries cut through Sharon, who was trying to steel herself from reacting. Emma longed to grab her cousin by the shoulders and demand why she was giving up her *kind* for a man who hadn't done anything but bellyache and eat prodigious amounts of food for the past four hours.

"I don't mean your kid," Ron shouted over the *boppli*'s pain-filled weeping. He still wore his coat, though it was warm in the apartment. There was a sheen of sweat on his forehead. "Though she needs to shut up."

Emma shot him a venomous glare, and he looked away. Was he a bully, too scared to face her? When she heard him curse under his breath, she knew pushing him would be as dangerous as trying to battle a lion with a chair and a whip.

"It's this snow," he went on. "We should have left hours ago." He slammed his hand against the wall, making the phone's bell jangle for the first time since Emma had moved in. She hadn't known there was a bell inside it.

"Well, we didn't." Sharon leaned into the arm of the sofa, her feet drawn up under her. She stared out the window at the curtain of snow that looked even colder in the dim light from the streetlamps at the front of the building. "Heading west would have taken us right into the storm.

Getting stuck in the mountains would have been dangerous."

"More dangerous than staying here?" he retorted, sitting at the table.

"What's dangerous here?" Sharon pulled a quilt over her lap and nestled under it. "We're warm, and Emma's got plenty of food." She glanced across the room. "You do, right?"

Emma continued holding Josie as the *boppli*'s howls faded into hiccuping sobs. "I'd planned to go grocery shopping in the morning, but we'll be fine if the storm lets up by midday tomorrow."

"If it doesn't?"

Emma didn't bother to answer Ron. It wasn't necessary. If the storm lasted longer than that, she'd have to figure out how to feed them. And she didn't want to say Josie was her first priority. The *boppli* must be fed. They could endure empty stomachs, but the little girl couldn't, not when she was ill.

She wasn't sure if her cousin or her fiancé would agree.

Ron growled an order to Sharon, who got up and went into the kitchen to explore the few cupboards and the fridge. Her face was drawn when she returned.

"Emma's right," she said. "There's not much."

"You told me the Ay-mish have plenty of food around. Why are you lying to me?" His hands closed into beefy fists.

Not wanting to see her cousin battered by his accusing words or worse, Emma replied, "*Ja*, Sharon is right. We have full cupboards after the harvest, but we just moved in here and haven't had a chance to plant a garden."

"You didn't bring anything from your other place?" he demanded, re-aiming his anger at her.

"No."

"Too bad. Those canned vegetables were tasty." As quickly as it had erupted, his fury dissipated. "Get me another sandwich, Sharon."

"There isn't any bread."

Ron puffed up like a snake, ready to spit venom in their direction. As he opened his mouth, a knock sounded on the exterior door.

Emma stopped dead in the midst of her pacing.

Closer to the kitchen, Sharon appeared paralyzed.

Ron jumped to his feet and ran to the door. Yanking it open, he shouted, "Who's there?"

Someone tall stepped out of the snow, seizing the edge of the door with a gloved hand. The shadowed form crumpled and collapsed in the entry. A pair of skis fell and clattered on the landing.

With a gasp, Emma shoved Josie into Sharon's arms. She ignored her cousin's protests and the *boppli*'s as she ran across the room and dropped to her knees beside Tyler. The skin on his face was chapped from cold and the wind.

What was he doing here? Had he lost every bit of his *gut* sense to go out into the storm?

She grasped his arm and tugged.

She couldn't move him.

She tried again.

No better, though a moan from Tyler made her heart fill with happiness. He was alive!

"Help me!" she ordered. "Ron, help me."

"Who is he?" Sharon's fiancé asked, shocking her that he was posing questions when snow was barraging them.

"Help me *now*!"

Her desperation, mixed with rage at their apparent indifference, added to her strength. Pulling on Tyler's arm again, she moved him a foot through the doorway. She shot a scowl at Ron, who seized Tyler's other arm and helped slide him into the room.

While someone closed the door—Emma didn't see who did it, but it must have been Sharon—she checked Tyler, who was face down on the floor. He was rigid with cold. She had to get these frozen clothes off him. Clawing at his ski clothes for any hold, she somehow managed to turn him onto his back. She unzipped his coat to let in the room's heat. Next, she unwrapped a hand-knitted scarf from around his neck and pulled off his hat and goggles. She tossed each onto the floor far enough from him so the cold emanating from them wouldn't flow over him.

"Who's this guy?" demanded Ron.

Emma didn't look up from trying to polish her glasses as the cold air turned to mist on them. "A member of our church."

"Doesn't look Ay-mish. I thought you rode around in buggies and wore old-fashioned clothes. Do all of you ski?"

She ignored him. "We need to get him warm."

Sharon asked from her other side, "What can I do to help?"

"Give me the quilt."

Her cousin pulled it off the sofa and held it out.

Taking it, Emma spread it over him. "Put the kettle on, Sharon. Fill it about half full of water. That way it'll heat up faster."

"Okay." She handed the *boppli* to Emma, then ran into the kitchen. Sounds of cast iron clanging against the stove emerged.

Hearing Ron walk toward the kitchen as he asked what else there was to eat, Emma bent toward Tyler and whispered, "Why did you think you could travel in this storm?"

He didn't answer her except to groan again. She prayed he'd revive soon. Then she could lambaste him for being foolish and apologize for the harsh words they'd exchanged earlier. She'd never been so anxious to say she was sorry.

Pain burning in his fingertips and toes was the first sensation Tyler could discern. The second was that he was lying on something hard. A road? No, the roads were covered by windblown drifts. A floor? How had he ended up flat on his back?

His eyes creaked open, then squeezed shut as light hit them. Squinting, he saw a welcome face leaning over him.

"Emma?" The question came out as a croak.

"Ja." She gazed down at him, along with Josie, who regarded him with tear-streaked cheeks.

"I got here!"

"Ja."

Puzzled by her terse answers, he pressed his hands against the floorboards and fought to sit. He doubted he would have managed it without her help. The quilt over him felt as heavy as a plow horse on his chest. His head spun, and he balanced it on his palms while he waited for the world to settle.

"Were you out of your mind to go out in this storm?" Emma asked as she sat on her heels.

He gave her a crooked smile. "I knew you'd need Josie's medicine."

"You brought it?"

"It's in my coat pocket. The zipper on the inside on the right."

She scrambled over to where the coat was spread out on the floor. She flipped it to the right side, then unzipped the inner pocket and pulled out the bottle.

"Is it frozen?" he asked.

Shaking the bottle, she said, "No. It seems to be okay." She stood. "Let me give it to Josie. Don't move."

If he didn't ache so bad, he might have laughed. Just thinking of moving hurt. He stared at the floor until Emma returned. She sat on her heels again, settling the *boppli* on her lap. He smiled at the *kind*, but that simple motion sent pain along his arms and legs.

"*Danki* for bringing the medicine," Emma said, "though you could have killed yourself in this storm."

"God guided me, helping me find the most direct route on my skis."

Her eyes widened, sending her ruddy eyebrows high above her glasses. "Cross-country skis? The ones you don't like?"

"Don't throw my stupid words back at me. I see now that cross-country skis have their uses. Like when the roads are snowed-in. I worried about you and Josie being by yourself." His smile faded as he realized for the first time that they weren't alone. An unfamiliar man and woman stood in the living room. "I guess I didn't need to fret about that."

"Tyler Lehman, my cousin, Sharon Miller, and her fiancé, Ron Timmerman. They stopped in to see me and *my* little Josie."

He heard the slight emphasis she put on the single word. Though he couldn't guess why she was pretending the *boppli* was hers and not her cousin's, he suspected the pretense had something to do with the man she'd called her cousin's fiancé. He noticed how stiffly she sat and how tightly she held Josie.

As if she was trying to protect the *kind*.

"Are you Ay-mish, too?" asked the other man.

Hoping he was doing the right thing, Tyler put on a tight smile, far less sincere, as he nodded. "That's nice you're visiting Emma, though you two didn't pick a great time to pay a call on her and her daughter. That storm doesn't show any sign of easing off anytime soon."

The other man slapped his hand on the table and cursed. "I told you we should have left hours ago."

"I know, Ron." Sharon held out a bowl.

Tyler couldn't see what was on it, but Ron grabbed it and sat at the table and began stuffing food into his mouth. Acting as if he wasn't paying any attention to the other man, Tyler got to his feet. His fingertips and toes were buzzing. Frostbite? He hoped not.

He accepted the cup Sharon held out to him and thanked her. It was *kaffi*, but without *millich*. No doubt, Emma had insisted they save whatever they had for Josie. Had she already retrieved what Dolly kept downstairs for her tea?

He was about to ask when the door to the interior stairs opened. He caught a glimpse of a flowered skirt and deep red sweater over it, but his eyes shifted when a chair crashed on the floor. Swiveling his head, he gasped.

Ron was on his feet, a gun in his hand that he was pointing at the door. Sharon shouted his name. When she moved toward him, he shoved her away with one burly hand.

"Whoa!" Dolly called from the doorway, holding her hands over her head. Her face was colorless beneath her mussed hair. "Put that away before someone gets hurt. I'm not breaking in. I own this building. I'm checking on Emma and the baby."

Ron motioned with the gun for Dolly to step inside. "Shut the door."

"Sure thing." She did as she cut her eyes toward Tyler and Emma, who was struggling to keep Josie from seeing what was going on.

Tyler knew Dolly was looking for answers. He wished he had some.

"Where's your phone?" Ron snapped.

Dolly touched the side of her long skirt. "In my pocket."

"Get it out. Toss it on the sofa."

She complied, her hands shaking so hard she sent the phone skittering across the floor.

"Ron!" Sharon cried as she ran to collect the phone, as her fiancé ordered. She gave it to him, and he turned it off before stuffing it into a pocket in his jeans. "Do as the lady says, Ron. Put the gun away."

"How do I know she's not a cop?"

Tyler kept his voice steady. "Dolly isn't a cop. She owns the store downstairs. If you want my guess—"

"I don't!" snapped Ron.

"—she's snowed in like the rest of us," he said, finishing, and knowing he needed to bring the room's tension level down a few thousand degrees before the man convinced himself to fire the gun.

"That's right." Dolly tried to smile but failed. "There's a car behind my truck. With the snow falling hard, I decided to stay and work. I fell asleep in the back room."

"Anyone else down there?" Ron's grip on the gun didn't ease.

"No. Just me. My husband was in a bad accident, and he hasn't been able to come to work."

Ron aimed the gun at Emma. "Is that true?"

"Ja." She half turned to keep herself between him and the *boppli*.

"Look at me!" he demanded. "Are you trying to hide a weapon?"

Sharon stepped forward. "They're Amish, Ron. They don't believe in violence. They won't fight, no matter what you do." Her eyes pleaded along with her words. "Instead, they'll pray for you and forgive you. There's no need to hurt them."

He gestured toward Dolly. "She's not one of them, is she?"

Emma answered before her cousin could. "Dolly is Tyler's *gut* friend. Tyler has been talking to her about our ways. That's what evangelical groups do when we hope someone will join us in our congregation."

Tyler hoped his shock was hidden. Nothing she'd said was true, but nothing was a lie, either. While working in the store, he, Emma and Dolly had talked about faith in addition to almost every other subject. Did Ron know Old Order Amish didn't reach out for new members? Unlikely, when he didn't know how to pronounce *Amish* correctly.

Dolly's breath slid out in a shuddering sigh when Ron lowered his gun and half turned while answering something Sharon had said. Tyler gasped. Past the open zipper on Ron's windbreaker, wads of cash were jammed. Tyler couldn't guess how much was hidden under his coat, but he doubted Ron had come by it honestly.

When he saw Emma's shocked expression, swiftly masked, he realized she'd also seen the money. She looked at him, and he shook his head as Ron closed his coat. Revealing they'd seen the cash would be dangerous.

"Over there." Again, Ron used the gun to emphasize his command. "Both of you."

Assuming he meant him and Emma, Tyler put

his arm around her shoulders and drew her a step toward his friend.

"No!" Ron screeched the single word. "The Ay-mish ski-guy and his hippie friend."

"Do as he asks," Emma said. "We'll be okay."

Though he wasn't sure anyone was safe, Tyler moved next to Dolly, whose face was as gray as the sky outside the window. He'd never felt so far from Emma and Josie. How stupid he'd been to waste the time they'd had together because he hadn't wanted to chance hurting her because of his own vacillation about baptism!

Save them, God. Please!

Emma held her breath as Tyler stood beside Dolly. The whole world seemed to be holding its breath. Snow continued to fall in silence, and her heart felt as if it didn't dare to beat. Sharon had halted her pleading with her fiancé. They waited for Ron's next move.

When he walked to the front of the room, keeping his gun aimed at the middle of Tyler's chest, she realized Ron was no longer paying attention to her and Josie. The *boppli* had fallen asleep on Emma's shoulder. Would Josie awaken if Emma moved? Knowing she had to take the chance, Emma took a single step to her left.

Nobody noticed. She slid farther along the wall as Ron pulled down a shade on one of the windows facing the street. He closed one, then swept the pistol in an arc at them before moving on to get the next. She kept her steps as slow as possible while she continued to edge away from him.

Her shoulder bumped into the wall phone. She moved in front of it and reached to lift the receiver. She held it close to the sleeping *boppli* to muffle the dial tone. It took every ounce of her flagging patience to wait until Ron's attention was focused on Sharon, who was berating him for being stupid for showing his weapon and threatening her cousin.

Emma tapped in 911 on the plastic buttons while she sang a lullaby to cover the sound of the soft beeps. Keeping the receiver against her chest, she altered the words to a request for help. She prayed her words would be audible through the crackling along the line, especially her request for the operator to remain silent.

How long did she have to convey the message?

While her cousin continued to remonstrate with Ron, Emma changed the lyrics to give their address and reveal that an armed man was threatening them. Would the operator comprehend the meaning behind her singing about a cat and mice in danger?

Then she heard a soft voice from the phone. It spoke a single word. "Understood."

Against her shoulder, Josie woke with a startled cry. Emma flinched, and the phone clicked against the wall unit.

Ron whirled to face her. Fear threatened to pin her to the wall, but she held out the cord for Josie to bat at with her tiny hands.

"Sorry," Emma said in a ragged whisper. "She catches it sometimes."

He stormed across the room. Beside Dolly, Tyler stiffened, but he didn't speak. They must wait like chess pieces and not move until they saw how Ron reacted.

Ron put his face close to hers. "Were you calling someone?"

"How?" Emma didn't want to lie, but she had to defuse his suspicions. "You took Dolly's phone."

"What about that one?"

As if in answer, the sound of a phone ringing downstairs in the shop seeped through the floorboards. The phone on the wall remained silent. Ron started to shove her aside and reach for the phone to check it, but halted when Sharon yelled his name.

"Don't hurt them, Ron!"

"I'm not going to hurt them," he retorted. "I want to know who she's been talking to."

Emma doubted anyone in the room believed him. Hoping she wasn't being foolish, she said, "I wasn't talking to anyone. It doesn't work. Check if for yourself and see."

"I don't believe you," Ron snarled. "Check it, Sharon!"

Her cousin walked over and grabbed the receiver out of Emma's hand. She pressed it to her ear, and Emma held her breath again as the phone continued to ring downstairs. The answering machine would pick up on the next ring. Could its message be heard through this receiver?

"Nothing!" Sharon ripped the cord out of the phone and tossed it aside. "What's going on, Ron? These people haven't done anything to you. Put the gun away."

"You're lying, too! You're both lying!" He grabbed Emma's arm. "Who did you call? The police?"

"Let her go." Tyler didn't raise his voice, though the cords along the sides of his neck popped out with strain.

"You don't give orders, Mr. Ay-mish!" Ron taunted, then put the gun close to Emma's face.

She closed her eyes. For so long, she'd feared she'd be the one left behind again, and she'd avoided risking her heart. When she heard the trigger click, she prayed Josie and the others would be saved.

"No!" Sharon's piercing cry rang through the room.

Emma was shoved aside, and fell to her knees. Josie screeched, but the *boppli*'s shrieks couldn't mute Sharon's voice.

"No, you can't shoot my baby!"

Chapter Fifteen

Everything went in fast forward and slow motion at the same time. Tyler wasn't sure how that was possible, but it's how it felt. Ron halted and didn't pull the trigger. Whether it was Sharon's cry or what she said that shocked him—or maybe both—he stared at her. At the same time, footsteps came flying up the stairs, inside and out.

Tyler ran on his painful feet to the exterior door and yanked it open, jumping aside in case the police fired. They didn't, as a trio of cops surged in like a spring flood. Dolly threw aside the door to the shop stairs. Within moments, the police had Ron disarmed and handcuffed. They did the same to Sharon when she protested his treatment.

While two police officers sat Sharon and Ron on the sofa and read them their rights before questioning them about an armed holdup at a gas station the previous night, a tall policewoman moved to where Dolly was embracing Emma and Josie. He longed to do the same, but the police officer gestured for them to follow her into the kitchen. Hooking a thumb toward Tyler, she gave a silent command for him to join them.

From behind him, Sharon shouted, "I didn't know, Emma! I was in the ladies' room. I didn't know he was going to rob the store."

Emma's shoulders grew taut, but she didn't answer.

Tyler kept his lips sealed, doubting he could restrain the question burning on his tongue. Was Sharon being honest or trying to save her skin?

"I'm Officer Flores," the policewoman said as she pulled out her phone and readied it to take notes.

He recognized the woman's name. His sister had spoken of meeting the officer when there had been some vandalism on a neighboring ranch last summer. Mollie had said Officer Flores was thorough and kind.

When she asked each of their full names, he noticed how Emma didn't hesitate on the *boppli*'s surname. Josie Miller.

The officer looked up. "You're not the baby's mother?"

"No, my cousin is."

"And your cousin is?"

"Sharon Miller." She pointed toward the sofa. "That's Sharon."

"Okay. The baby's hers?"

"*Ja*, but she gave me the necessary paperwork tonight to transfer custody."

Tyler heard the happiness and gratitude in her voice. His heart flooded with joy for her. And for him, though he might have messed up every opportunity to remain a part of their lives.

Officer Flores rolled her eyes. "Let's not make this any more complicated than it has to be. The baby belongs to her, right?"

"*Ja*."

"She and the baby live with you?"

"No, just Josie. Sharon left her with me a year ago when we were traveling west. I haven't seen Sharon again until this evening."

The police officer nodded. "Okay. Let's deal with one issue at a time. Tell me what occurred from when you walked in, Emma, and found those two."

Tyler listened to Emma explain. She stuck to the facts, but emotion underlined each word she spoke. He couldn't forget Sharon had been Emma's way to escape her cruel *aenti*, and it must be breaking her heart to see her cousin involved in a crime. Wanting to take Emma into his arms and offer her comfort, he instead prayed for God to keep sending her the strength she needed to get through what was to *komm*.

Then it was his turn. What he related was much shorter, because Emma had been with her cousin and her fiancé for hours while Tyler was fighting his way through the snow. As he shared his experiences, he wished his *kaffi* wasn't getting cold on the table. Though the chill deep within him had more to do with what had happened inside the apartment than outside.

Then, Dolly completed her own explanation when she said simply, "Wrong place, wrong time."

Finishing her notes, Officer Flores looked at Emma. "As for this baby, we're going to need a social worker to get this straightened out. I suggest we get your bishop in on this. He's a good guy for handling ticklish situations, and this one's a doozy." She eyed them. "You need to come to the station tomorrow to give an official statement. By then, the streets should have been plowed." She glanced at her phone again. "I've got all I need for now. Any questions for me?"

Tyler was about to shake his head, but halted when Emma asked in a small voice, "Can Josie stay with me for now?"

"Let me check."

Emma put her hand over her mouth as if she was about to be ill. Tyler understood her reaction. As bad as it was to see her cousin in handcuffs, the idea of the *boppli* being taken away was many times worse.

Officer Flores moved away to make a call. Nothing in her pose gave any hint to what she was saying and what she was hearing.

"Which one of you is Dolly?" asked another cop, who had come into the apartment from the inside stairs.

"I am." Dolly raised a shaking hand.

"Call for you. From your husband." He thrust a phone into her hand. Tyler recognized it as the handset from the shop.

"Gil!" She hit the speaker button. "We're safe."

"Why aren't you answering your cell?" Gil's demanding voice asked. "Why is a policeman answering the shop phone? I've been calling and calling."

Tyler smiled as his friend kept peppering Dolly with questions, not giving her a chance to answer. Gil was going to be impossible to be around when he learned his persistent calls had protected Emma by convincing Ron—just long enough—that the phone upstairs didn't work.

"I'm glad that this one time," Emma murmured beneath Dolly's attempts to soothe her husband, "Gil was too distracted to do what he'd promised. If he'd unhooked the phone..." She paused as she realized the *boppli* had fallen asleep again.

He held out his arms, and Emma put Josie in them. The little girl murmured something in her dreams and nuzzled up close to him. Tears rose in his eyes as he thought of how close death had been to the *kind*.

"It's okay," Emma said. "We're safe. At least

for now." Her face hardened with dread as Officer Flores returned to where they stood.

"Here's the deal. The roads are closed, so nobody's coming to take custody of the child right now. I don't see any choice but to leave her with you." Officer Flores lowered her professional façade enough to smile. "That's what I have to say. What I *want* to say is you've been taking care of that little girl for a year now, and anyone can see she's thriving." She became somber again. "The Colorado Department of Human Services will have to get involved. Possibly the folks in Ohio. You'll be assigned a social worker, and he or she will determine where Josie lives in the future and with whom. You understand it wouldn't be seen as a positive thing if you and the baby were to leave. Got it?"

"I understand," Emma said, her voice trembling. Then she smiled and put her hand on the *boppli*'s back.

Tyler wondered if she felt the same connection he did as they stood in the eye of the hurricane around them. It was one he didn't want to break.

Not ever.

Emma wanted to drop to her knees and shout out her thanks to God. She wanted to fling her arms around Tyler while she celebrated these blessed tidings with him. When she saw the intense emotions in his eyes as they caught hers, she wanted to forget everything but this moment.

She couldn't. She had to think of Josie. "What should I do next, Officer Flores?"

"I don't know much about custody issues, but I'd hold on to any paperwork you've got and have it ready for the social worker to go through." The policewoman's voice softened. "I wish I could help you more. Let me know if there's anything I can do." Her dark gaze swept from her to Tyler and Dolly, who was sitting at the dining-room table, talking with Gil, but now without the speaker on. "I'll see you tomorrow at the station."

Emma almost begged for clemency for her cousin. She bit her lower lip before the words could slip out. Keeping the police from doing their job wouldn't be the best way to help Sharon.

Dolly came over to them while the cops herded their prisoners out. Snow and icy wind swirled into the apartment. She batted it away as she said, "We'll find her a good lawyer."

Emma wasn't surprised Dolly had guessed what she'd been thinking. "I may need one, too," she said under her breath.

Tyler must have heard her because he frowned. "Why would you need a lawyer, Emma? You weren't involved in their crimes."

"If Sharon changes her mind and wants Josie back—"

"Let's deal with one problem at a time." Dolly

patted her shoulder. "Anyone can see you're a much better mother for Josie than her real mother is."

Emma flinched when she heard how Dolly described Sharon. Would the social worker feel the same? That Emma wasn't a *real* parent?

Dolly's phone rang again. "Gil. He's downstairs. You know he's not going to want to miss the excitement."

She nodded, understanding what Dolly hadn't said. Gil hadn't let his cast keep him from getting to the shop to make sure his wife was okay. The sight of police vehicles next to the shop must have been horrifying for him. "Let Gil know we're all okay."

"I'll be in for work tomorrow," Tyler added. "Actually today. Getting home won't be easy or quick."

"That's a good idea, Tyler." Dolly took a deep breath. "What's left of this adrenaline might as well be put to work finishing up the last items on the to-do list, so we can open as planned."

She threw open the door to the interior stairs and rushed out. Emma heard the stairs squeak as Dolly hurried down. Light flashed on the snow as she hit every switch downstairs. Then came the exultant sound of Gil crying out her name.

Emma smiled as she imagined their eager embrace. The Yarwoods had been kind to her and

Josie. That Dolly had been put in danger because of her made her feel nauseated again.

"*You* didn't do anything wrong tonight." Tyler's tender voice drew her from the precipice of her thoughts. He set a once-again awake Josie on the sofa and handed her toys. "Except let my *kaffi* go cold."

She laughed at his teasing attempt to free her from her grim feelings. "I saw your reaction when you got it with no *millich*. Sharon could barely swallow hers without it."

"You didn't tell them about the refrigerator downstairs, ain't so?"

"I had no idea how long we'd be snowbound, and Josie would need *millich*." The sounds of a heavy box being dragged along the floor below and the thump of crutches interrupted her. Smiling, she went on. "Dolly's going to be thrilled with Gil helping her finish her jobs list." She walked over to where Josie sat with her favorite book in her hands as she turned the thick pages. That the book was upside down didn't seem to faze the *boppli*. "I wonder how long his enthusiasm for the store will last when he's well enough to head out on his bike again. Do you think he'll change and be more helpful to her instead of rushing off to find the next big thing?"

Tyler raised his eyebrows. "What happened tonight is the sort of experience that changes a man. I've never heard Gil sound as frightened as he did tonight."

"Which doesn't answer my question. Do you think Gil will see how he needs to balance work, fun and family instead of depending on Dolly to handle everything?"

"I'll answer that question if you'll answer one for me."

She started to agree, but Josie threw the book on the floor and let out a frustrated wail. It was such a normal reaction that Emma almost burst into tears, relieved the little girl was safe and with her. At least for now. She had to stop worrying about what *might* happen and be grateful for what *was* happening.

After putting Josie in her high chair, Emma handed her a teething biscuit. As the *boppli* chewed on it, Emma said, "I'll answer a question for you, but you answer my question first. I want your opinion on this." She folded her arms in front of her, gripping her elbows in an effort not to fall apart in front of Tyler. Tears burned her throat, and her fingers and knees seemed determined to shake now that the worst of the confrontation was over and Ron couldn't injure the people about whom she cared most.

"That sounds fair." He crossed the room and put his hand on Josie's chair. "You're wondering if Gil has seen the foolishness of his ways and will start to appreciate how Dolly has supported his dreams."

"*Ja.*"

"I wish I could give you the answer I know you want."

"Dolly has done everything she can to make the shop a success. Twice."

"I know."

"How can he expect her to do more?"

He shook his head. "You're asking the wrong person. Only Gil can answer that, but knowing my friend, I believe he's seeing at last what should come first in his life. It's not easy to realize you've failed to tell the most important person in your life how much they mean to you and you may never have another opportunity."

Emma stared at him. Was he talking about Gil and Dolly now or about himself and her?

Before she could find a way to ask such a question, Tyler said, "My turn to get my question answered. That's what you agreed to, ain't so?"

"*Ja.*"

"You'll answer it honestly?"

Her eyes widened. "Of course! How can you…?" She bit off the rest of the words when his mouth twitched as he fought a smile. Abruptly, the tremors rippling through her weren't the residue of fear but her longing for his kiss.

He held out his hand without speaking. She was just as silent as she put her own in his. As his fingers closed around hers, she walked with him toward one of the front windows. He raised the shade to reveal the falling snow.

The police cars had vanished, leaving a crisscross of tire marks in the snow. Each streetlight wore a bright white cap that grew higher with every flake that fell upon it. Nobody was visible on the street, but within great squares of light spilling from the shop below, the silhouettes of the Yarwoods working together in a silent choreography could be seen.

Tyler stepped behind her and wrapped her arms and his around her. She rested her head against him, delighting in his heart's steady thump. As she gazed out at the bucolic winter scene, she let go of the terror that had held her prisoner.

She couldn't have said how long they stood like that in perfect silence and harmony. For once, she didn't ponder how long it would last. She basked in every breath she drew because each was flavored with the scent of his soap.

When he spoke, she sighed. Not because she was unhappy, but because she adored his rough but gentle tone and how his words brushed past her ear in a fleeting caress.

"Gil isn't the only one tonight," he whispered, "who's learned the lesson about keeping an eye on what and who are most important in your life. I've learned it. While I was skiing through the storm, telling God I'd do whatever He wished if He would let me get to you—"

She spun within his arms to face him. "You know prayer doesn't work like that, ain't so? It's a supplication, not a bartering session."

"I know that. I'm explaining it wrong. I didn't negotiate with God. I put myself in His hands and asked for His help because I wanted to be able to get Josie's medicine to you." He brushed his fingers against her cheek. "To let you know how wrong I was to insist you must feel a certain way about your cousin and Josie and everything else. I should know better because I avoid letting others try to convince me what to do. You've spent your life with someone else telling you what to do and say and feel."

"*Ja.*"

"Tonight I saw you stand up to someone determined to bend you to his will." He tipped her chin toward him. "There was one thing your *aenti* couldn't force out of you. Your compassionate heart. Everything you did tonight was intended to protect those you care about."

"I haven't said how much I appreciate you bringing Josie's medicine." She pressed her hand to the front of his shirt. "Though you were a *dummkopf* to risk your life."

"I can't argue with that." His fingers curved along her jaw, brushing her ear as his words had. "Okay, you told me you'd answer one question.

Before I ask that question, there's something you need to know. Though I've fought it, I've fallen in love with you."

"I've fallen in love with you, too." She didn't add that she'd been struggling as well, not wanting to believe she deserved such happiness.

"I haven't said anything because I didn't want to drag you into my messed-up life. A grown man who hasn't decided what he wants to be when he grows up."

"I didn't hear a question. Did you ask one?"

"No. Not yet." He stepped back and took her hands in his. "Emma, you're *wunderbaar*. You're worth more than the rest of the world to me."

She pressed her hands over her lips, but a gasp burst past them. "My *daed* used to say that when he was tucking me in. He'd tell me he wouldn't trade the whole of the world for me."

"Your *daed* knew what was important in life." He drew her hands down and folded them between his again. "Emma, I love you more than anything else in the world." He grinned. "With Josie a close second. Tell me you'll marry me."

"Marry you?"

"*Ja.*" He caressed her lips with his own, and everything she'd been unsure about fell into place.

"You never asked me that question," she said.

"I didn't. All right. Here goes." He chuckled. "How long do you think it'll take you to learn to stand up on your skis for more than a minute or two?"

Startled at the unexpected change of subject, she stuttered, "I—I don't know."

"An honest answer, and I'll give you another honest answer. If it takes me the rest of my life to find out, that's okay with me. Will you be my wife, Emma, and give me a lifetime of happiness?" He kissed her again, once more a swift touch that left her longing for more. "Before you answer, you should know I did *komm* to an understanding with God tonight. I told Him how much I love you, and He reminded me how much He loves His *kinder*, including me. I lost one *daed* on Earth, but not my Heavenly *Daed*. He has been there for me, even when I was at my most stubborn. I want to acknowledge my connection with Him, and I want to show everyone my love for you. Will you marry me, so you and I and Josie can be a family?"

"*Ja*. A thousand times *ja*."

He swept her into his arms, and the kiss they shared was sweet and slow and wondrous.

Epilogue

Emma sat on the backless bench in the Lehmans' house near the end of July. The furniture had been cleared out of the living room and replaced with benches for the *Leit*'s worship. Men and women faced each other, and the elderly sat in kitchen chairs closest to where the bishop had asked them to bow their heads in prayer.

Her hands were around Josie, who was curled up on her lap. The little girl had fallen asleep about half an hour ago after crying because she couldn't go into the laundry room with Tyler. No one but the ordained men were allowed in with the baptism candidates. The bishop had gone in to talk with them while the *Leit* sang a long hymn, but had returned to stand at the ends of the rows of benches.

Two young men and a young woman, hardly more than teenagers, walked out of the room. Tyler brought up the end of the line. When his gaze met and melded with hers, she imagined another day in the not-too-distance future when she and Tyler would stand in front of the *Leit* and speak their vows to love and cherish each other for the rest of their lives.

"See Tyler?" she whispered to Josie, who bounced on her lap with excitement at seeing the man she adored and was already calling "Dada." Only last week the *boppli* had called her *Mamm* for the first time. There was still a bunch of hoops to jump through before she could adopt Josie. Before she and Tyler could. Though the social worker hadn't said, Emma knew being a married couple would add credibility to their plans to raise Josie.

Tyler kneeled in front of the row of ordained men, their two ministers, their deacon and the bishop. Jerek Stahl, their bishop, was the shortest of the quartet. His beard was as thin as he was, but he wasn't a man to dismiss quickly. His strength was from within and shone out of his dark eyes.

Jerek took a handful of water from the container the deacon held, then placed his cupped hands on Tyler's head. After asking if Tyler was ready to commit his life to God and their community and hearing Tyler's clear answers, he opened his hands to let the water wash down over Tyler's head. Jerek did the same with each of the others seeking baptism. They each were now an integral part of the community, sewn to it with invisible threads that must never be broken.

As she watched, Emma thanked God for bringing them to this day. Tyler would never become a conventional Amish man, because he planned to continue to work for the Yarwoods, but then she wasn't a conventional Amish woman, either. She'd headed off across the country on a whim and had with God's grace made a life for herself in a place where she hadn't known a soul.

As the long service came to an end and everyone helped prepare for the communal meal, Emma gave up trying to reach Tyler to congratulate him. He glanced in her direction, then shrugged as he was surrounded by the men who had known him his whole life and were thrilled he'd taken his place among them.

Emma's steps as she walked out onto the porch faltered when she saw a familiar form standing by the road. Sharon! Though she'd known her cousin had been released from jail because she had been ignorant of her erstwhile fiancé's crimes in Lost River and in Ohio, Emma hadn't spoken with Sharon since the horrible night of the spring blizzard.

Sharon walked toward her. She wasn't dressed plain, but also wasn't wearing fashionable *Englisch* clothing. Her dress was simple, and she wore her hair in a bun. No *kapp* covered it.

"I'm heading home to Ohio," Sharon said without meeting her eyes.

"Alone?"

"If you mean Ron, I'll be happy if I never see him again, though I've been told I'll be called as a witness at his trials."

Emma hesitated, then asked, "Is it okay for you to leave Colorado?"

"I've gotten permission from the court. They let me know if I don't show up for court, they'll throw the book at me."

"What are you going to do in Ohio?"

"I'm going to stay with an old friend. She's been ill, and she needs someone to cook and clean." She hesitated, then asked, "How is everything going for you to adopt Josie?"

"A lot of paperwork, but the social worker is guiding us through it."

"I'm glad." She reached out a single finger toward the little girl. When Josie grabbed it, a smile fled across Sharon's lips. She blinked hard as she drew her finger away as if the contact had been painful. "She deserves a family. A good family, ain't so?"

Emma nodded, unable to speak as she heard her cousin use the familiar phrase. Sharon hadn't said if her friend was plain or *Englisch*. Not that it mattered because, Emma hoped, that friend was giving Sharon a chance to remake her life with *gut* decisions…at last.

"Will you visit us when you return for the trial?"

"I may." Her tone suggested she wouldn't, that

she wanted to put her daughter and her cousin and everything else to do with Lost River far in her past.

Emma understood that because she'd tried to do the same thing with her anger with her *aenti* and her grief about her parents. Last month, with the bishop's guidance, she'd written a letter to *Aenti* Pearl to say where she was and what she was doing. She'd expected a terse response or maybe none at all. Instead, she'd received a heartfelt missive about how glad her *aenti* was that she'd found happiness. There hadn't been any hint of an invitation to call if she was ever in Indiana. However, Emma suspected if she did, her *aenti* would open her door as long as Emma wasn't planning on staying.

"I hope you will visit us," Tyler said as he came over to them. "A *kind* can't have too many people who love her."

Sharon nodded and walked toward a car marked as a ride-share vehicle. She got in. The car drove off, raising a cloud of dust.

"*Danki*, Tyler," Emma said. "Maybe she'll heed your invitation."

"She will or she won't. Only God knows what's to *komm*, which is why we're often surprised."

"Like you were by the instant success of Dolly and Gil's shop?"

He shook his head. "No, that wasn't a surprise. The bakery was successful until Gil got it in his mind that they should have a sports-equipment shop. They were so successful they had to hire my *mamm* to make pies for them."

"Dolly will handle the baking in Pagosa Springs." Emma hadn't been the only one astonished to learn Gil's negotiations in the city in the San Juan Mountains had been for a space where Dolly could open a restaurant that would serve only lunch and dinner, so she didn't have to get out of bed in the middle of the night. That there were many bike trails in the area had also helped Gil decide they should move there. Mountain Sports and Adventures would be managed by Tyler, and he would move into the upstairs apartment after he and Emma were married.

"*Ja.* Dolly's looking forward to it." He grinned. "She's assured me she'll be happy to keep baking for us because they've hired a chef to handle most of the cooking for the restaurant while she spends her time with her customers."

"That will make Dolly very happy."

"Which makes Gil happy." He paused and cleared his throat.

"Emma, there's something we need to talk about."

"What?"

"Not here."

He lifted Josie out of Emma's arms, then set her on the ground. They each took one of the *kind*'s hands as they walked toward the large cottonwood that shaded the house where he'd grown up. They walked at the little girl's pace.

Once they were on the far side of the porch, he said, "Nick Bakke contacted me last week and asked if I'd be interested in doing vacation relief for members of the ski patrol at Bison Springs Resort."

"What did you tell him?" she asked, hardly daring to breathe.

"That I'd need to discuss it with my soon-to-be wife. Or should I say not-soon-enough-to-be wife?" He drew her behind a thick tree and clasped his hands behind her waist. Josie toddled after them, throwing her arms around his leg. "I don't need to ask, though. I'd rather spend my time here with you." With a saucy grin, he said, "Kolton and the fire chief have convinced me if I want to help others here in the valley, I can do that by joining the fire department."

She remembered his astonishment at how well the firefighters had worked to keep the fire at the cabin from spreading and how Chet had told him to drop in and see him. She searched his face and saw serving others in the plain community and beyond was the life he was meant to have. "That's a *gut* plan," she said and realized she meant it.

"Between managing the shop and taking fire-fighter training, I won't have much spare time this summer. However, by the time the snow flies again, I'd like to see if I can get you up on skis for more than thirty seconds at a time."

"I don't know if skiing well is something I'll ever be able to do," she said with a smile. "I'm willing to try if you are."

"I am, even if it takes a lifetime. Maybe especially if it takes a lifetime—a lifetime with you."

As she met his lips with her own, she knew in each other's arms was the place they'd been seeking. Her journey alone was over, and she'd reached its destination, but her journey with him was just beginning.

* * * * *

Dear Reader,

Welcome back to the San Luis Valley of south-central Colorado. Some people can go to a new place and find a home, while others, who have been born and raised there, can't wait to get out. Emma Weaver never planned to be on her own with a baby, and she thinks she can handle everything. At the same time, Tyler Lehman looks around the familiar valley and wonders if he belongs there. They are dealing with life-changing questions, and they've got to learn that, with God's help, they can find the answers together. It's easy for all of us to think we can do everything on our own, but we all need help. From our friends and family and from God.

Visit me at www.joannbrownbooks.com. And look for my next book in the Amish of Lost River series, coming soon!

Wishing you many blessings,
Jo Ann Brown